Acclaim for Trio Sonata

"This is one of the most beautifully written books I have come across in years. Juliet Sarkessian is surely destined to become one of our greatest writing talents."

—Greg Herren, Former Editor,
Lambda Book Report

"While other writers attempt to pin love down, Juliet Sarkessian has the confidence to let her subject float and flutter, revealing its many colors in elusive motion. This is a brave and remarkably generous novel."

—Jim Gladstone, Author,
The Big Book of Misunderstanding

"Daringly incorrect politically . . . a close look at an erotic relationship between a straight woman and two gay men."

—Patricia Nell Warren, Author,
The Front Runner and *Billy's Boy*

Trio Sonata

HARRINGTON PARK PRESS
Southern Tier Editions
Gay Men's Fiction
Jay Quinn, Executive Editor

Love, the Magician by Brian Bouldrey

Distortion by Stephen Beachy

The City Kid by Paul Reidinger

Rebel Yell: Stories by Contemporary Southern Gay Authors edited by Jay Quinn

Rebel Yell 2: More Stories of Contemporary Southern Gay Men edited by Jay Quinn

Metes and Bounds by Jay Quinn

The Limits of Pleasure by Daniel M. Jaffe

The Big Book of Misunderstanding by Jim Gladstone

This Thing Called Courage: South Boston Stories by J. G. Hayes

Edge by Jeff Mann

Trio Sonata by Juliet Sarkessian

Bear Like Me by Jonathan Cohen

Goneaway Road by Dale Edgerton

The Concrete Sky by Marshall Moore

Through It Came Bright Colors by Trebor Healey

Elf Child by David M. Pierce

Huddle by Dan Boyle

The Man Pilot by James W. Ridout IV

Edge by Jeff Mann

Ambidextrous: The Secret Lives of Children by Felice Picano

Men Who Loved Me by Felice Picano

A House on the Ocean, A House on the Bay by Felice Picano

Trio Sonata

Juliet Sarkessian

Southern Tier Editions
Harrington Park Press®
An Imprint of The Haworth Press, Inc.
New York • London • Oxford

Published by

Southern Tier Editions, Harrington Park Press®, an imprint of The Haworth Press, Inc., 10 Alice Street, Binghamton, NY 13904-1580.

PUBLISHER'S NOTE
This is a work of fiction. Names, characters, places, and incidents either are the products of the author's imagination or are used fictitiously, and any resemblance to actual persons, living or dead, business establishments, events, or locales is entirely coincidental.

Cover design by Raymond E. Mingst.

Library of Congress Cataloging-in-Publication Data

Sarkessian, Juliet.
    Trio sonata : a novel / by Juliet Sarkessian.
        p. cm.
    ISBN 1-56023-401-6 (alk. paper)—ISBN 1-56023-402-4 (soft)
    1. Triangles (Interpersonal relations)—Fiction. 2. Philadelphia (Pa.)—Fiction. 3. Heterosexual women—Fiction. 4. Violinists—Fiction. 5. Gay men—Fiction. I. Title.

PS3619.A74 T75 2002
813'.6—dc21

2002069056

Chapters

Acknowledgments

Trio Sonata would never have been completed without the help and support of my partner, Nena, who acted as my first editor, taught me how to write like an adult, and fills my life with love. Incalculable thanks are also due to Jay Quinn, my editor and champion, without whom this book would still be in my dresser. I am also indebted to Greg Herren and Paul Willis for opening doors; Amelia Zalcman for heading me in the right direction; Raymond Mingst for a brilliant cover design and incisive comments; Heather Jones Gay for editorial assistance in the early stages; Joan Hoffman, my first and most enthusiastic reader; Bettie Eskridge, Debbie Hoover, Laura Hall Zucker, and Lisa Work for their comments and encouragement; Jessica Lustig, for the window she provided on the world of classical musicians; and Karen Zweizig Naghski for correcting my French. Additional thanks go out to Pedro Angel Figueredo, Augustine Garcia Lopez, and David Tasker. This book is dedicated to the memory of my classmates Joseph Widowfield and Tim Collier, who died too young, and to the memory of my grandmothers, Zabel Indjehagopian Hachikian and Maquouhe Fereshetian Sarkessian, who inspire me every day of my life.

Prelude

For her, it was the beginning of time. Before that there were only vague recollections of the color and pattern of bathroom tile, the smell of paste, an image of children's drawings on a nursery-room wall, a sense of being trapped in a small wooden crib, the excitement of being twirled in the air above an adult's head, a feeling of loneliness associated with a playground bench and a metal sliding board.

Janna was four when it happened. In her mind's eye she views the scene as if she were an outsider, standing at a safe distance. They were on their way home from nursery school in the backseat of a car driven by a woman she no longer remembers. Janna was sitting quietly between the boys when they began to pull down her slacks and underpants. She sees herself in that ugly corduroy bonnet her mother made her wear, so terrified and humiliated she couldn't move or speak. They didn't touch her. They only looked and laughed. Her cousin, also in the back and then only three, began hitting the boy closest to him. The commotion caused the carpool mother to yell over her shoulder at them, but she never turned around to see what was going on.

That evening, when Janna's mother was getting her ready for bed, Janna told her what had happened. She expected her mom to be angry at the boys for what they had done. Instead, she asked Janna why she hadn't said anything to the driver when it was happening. The message was clear, even to a four-year-old. But it didn't matter what her mother thought, because Janna knew it was not her fault.

Years later she attended high school with these boys. She went out of her way to avoid them, afraid they would say something about the incident that would revive her sense of shame and power-lessness. Yet it bothered her that they never acknowledged, let alone apologized for, what they had done. Janna wondered if they even remembered who she was. The event was undoubtedly mean-ingless to them. But it would remain etched in Janna's memory for-ever.

Romance

Janna walked briskly through the grime of Chestnut Street, past Islamic merchants, their tables full of pungent, burning incense, past the bus stops crowded with office workers on their way home, past the shoe stores and discount pharmacies. Her briefcase banged incessantly against her calf, an irksome reminder of how poorly the meeting with her loan officer had gone. He left her with little choice. Either she had to forgo her plans to expand her café, or she had to mortgage her home to finance it. The decision she had hoped to avoid was now imminent.

Janna stepped onto a quiet side street, slowing her pace. The warmth of the late afternoon sun soaked her face and arms, helping her to forget, at least momentarily, her financial troubles. She watched her feet break lazily through shadows of leaves and branches cast on the uneven brick sidewalk. She was now in the part of Philadelphia she loved best, full of quaint town houses with shuttered windows and decorative iron work, some on streets so old they had posts for tethering horses. Janna peered into windows as she passed them. Here a family sat down to dinner, there a woman worked at a computer, and on the stoop of an old building a young couple leashed their dog for a walk. Other people's lives always looked so inviting from this distance. She wished she could try on each one until she found the perfect fit, full of noisy excitement and quiet joy.

Turning onto Pine Street from Seventeenth, she approached her café. Elizabeth, her employee, was still inside, but the "Closed" sign was in the window. Janna fumbled through her purse for the keys. As she unlocked the door, she heard a voice behind her. She turned to find a young man holding a key that had fallen from her chain.

He handed it to her and she thanked him. As she watched him walk away, she thought how she missed being that young.

◆◆◆

Winston held out Janna's seat in the front box of the Academy of Music, then sat beside her. He looked good this evening, Janna thought, less haggard than usual. "I'm sorry we have to do this tonight," he said, "but as dean, I thought I should make an appearance."

"Don't apologize. I love premieres."

"His concerto is first. We should be out of here within the hour."

Janna sat back and watched as the seats around them filled up. She recalled the excitement of her first time here. She was twelve, and her grandparents had brought her to see *Coppelia*. The inside of the Academy was like a jewel box, all bright lights and gold leaf. The women, their hair swept up with pretty clips and combs, were dressed in sparkling clothes, carrying beaded purses and fancy opera glasses. As a child, Janna had leaned over the third-tier balcony, dreaming of someday being one of those women, sitting like royalty in the curved box next to the stage, the very one she was in now. She was disappointed when she finally got to sit in the box. Regardless of how she angled her chair, half of the stage was blocked from her view. Since that time she avoided these seats whenever possible, but tonight she had no choice.

"This is a good turnout for the Curtis Orchestra," Janna said, flipping through her program. "Are they all here to see him?"

He nodded. "We're lucky he chose Curtis over Juilliard. He certainly had his pick. He's a major talent, a brilliant young composer and an extraordinary violinist. He's the fair-haired child of the administration." He hesitated, then added, "Deservedly so."

As Winston spoke, Janna noticed his hands fidgeting with the cover of his program, folding a corner in overlapping triangles of increasing size. She recalled their first date, when he had told her of his youthful ambition to become a composer. After years passed without recognition, he began doubting his abilities and eventually abandoned his artistic aspirations for the relative safety of an academic career. His willingness to confide this sense of failure to Janna was what first drew her to him. She took his hand. "You said you had something special planned tonight. Tell me about it."

He perked up. "It's a surprise, for your birthday. You'll have to wait."

It was hard for Janna to believe she was turning thirty. She thought it silly that this particular year of one's life was treated as such a milestone but got caught up in the myth of it anyway. In a few months it would be 1990, the start of the last decade of the century. She wondered where she'd be in ten years, when the new millennium was about to begin. The thought of it made her frightened and depressed. It was not the way she wanted to feel tonight. She forced a smile. "I'm sure whatever you have planned will be wonderful."

The lights dimmed. The audience applauded as the conductor approached the podium. He was followed by a young man carrying a violin. Tall and gawky, he couldn't have been more than nineteen. A bow tie of white silk, knotted below a prominent Adam's apple, provided a sharp contrast to his deep blue eyes and dark hair. Janna found him remarkably poised for someone so young. The audience grew quiet as he took his place at the front of the orchestra. The concerto opened with a lone bassoon, a sad, mysterious sound, like a foghorn at sea. Slowly, other sections of the orchestra joined in. Then, raising his violin, the composer began a delicate and eerie melody that twisted through a profusion of minor chords. Although Janna knew she could not have heard this music before, it seemed deeply familiar, as if the composer had reached into the collective human memory and recovered an ancient, long-forgotten dirge. The piece closed as it had begun, with the melancholy sound of the bassoon drifting off into the night.

The audience applauded, although not with the degree of enthusiasm Janna believed the work warranted. Nevertheless, the young composer seemed pleased as he bowed and smiled. He left the stage and the lights went up for intermission. The audience rustled in their seats, searching for their programs and pocketbooks.

Janna and Winston went to a reception area backstage. As they waited for the composer, Winston made his rounds among other faculty members from Curtis. After a few minutes, the composer emerged in the company of another young man. They were both dazzling in tuxedos and wide, unaffected grins. Janna stifled a laugh when she saw the composer's hair. It was sticking up in clumps, like someone had affectionately run a hand through it. Janna eyed the man standing so close to him as to be nearly touching. He was handsome, with dark hair and eyes, and a crisp dimple that appeared in the center of one cheek every time he smiled. He looked a year or two older than the composer and, at six feet, a few inches shorter. There was something familiar about him. Janna asked Winston if he was a Curtis student, but he didn't recognize him.

A stern-looking older couple were the first to approach the composer, the man in a well-worn tuxedo, the woman in an ill-fitting tweed suit. "Who are they?" Janna asked.

"The parents. The father's a first violinist in the Philadelphia Orchestra. The mother's a musicologist. She's a real piece of work." Other people approached the composer, shaking his hand and patting him on the back. His companion spoke to a few of the students but otherwise stood out of the way. After the well-wishers had dispersed, Winston and Janna came forward. Winston shook the composer's hand vigorously. "Well done, young man, well done." He turned to Janna. "This is Alex Everett. Alex, Janna."

Alex smiled warmly and extended his hand. "Very nice to meet you." He drew his companion forward. "This is Philip."

The young man shook Winston's hand first, then Janna's. "We meet again," he said to her with playful mystery.

"I thought I recognized you, but I'm embarrassed to say I can't remember from where."

"You dropped your key. I picked it up."

"That's right. What a funny coincidence."

"Shades of *La Bohème,*" Alex said with a raised eyebrow.

Looking at the two of them, Janna had a feeling Mimi would have a very small role in this production. She turned her attention to the composer. "The concerto was astonishing. That moment, when the music was about to reach a crescendo, and the entire orchestra stopped—it was like I could reach out and touch the silence, it was so real."

"The conductor and orchestra deserve credit for that."

"Not only brilliant, but modest, too. Well, thank you for creating music that's original *and* accessible."

"Accessible." Alex grinned. "Now there's a dirty word."

"Not to everyone."

"I'm glad you enjoyed it."

Janna turned to the other young man. "Do you go to Curtis too?"

He chuckled. She noticed his long lashes, the only soft note on an otherwise masculine face. "No. I'm an engineering student at Drexel."

Janna glanced knowingly at Alex, pursing her lips. "Good catch."

Alex blushed a little and smiled but stopped when he saw the uncomfortable look on his dean's face. Strains of Khatchaturian's *Masquerade* reached them from the auditorium. "We shouldn't keep you from the rest of the performance," Alex offered graciously.

"We only came for your piece," Janna replied.

"We do have dinner plans, though," Winston interjected, "so I'm afraid we'll have to be on our way." He reached out and shook Alex's hand again. "Keep up the good work." He gave Philip a tense smile, then moved away.

Janna extended her hand, first to Alex, then to Philip. "It's been a pleasure meeting you both. I hope we'll have the chance to see each other again soon."

Janna stepped out of the Academy and stood for a moment at the top of the stone staircase. She welcomed the burst of cold air that whipped her hair behind her like a ragged sail in a storm. Filled with a newfound sense of excitement, she descended the steps toward Winston. "Where to next?" she asked.

He glared at her suspiciously. "How do you know that guy?"

"What guy?"

"My student's friend."

"Oh, a few weeks ago I dropped a key outside the café. He was there, so he handed it to me." Winston looked unconvinced. "Please don't tell me you're jealous. Besides being ten years younger than me, he's clearly that boy's lover."

A curdled expression crept across Winston's face. "Now that's something I'd rather not think about."

"No one's asking you to think about it," Janna replied tersely as she pulled her wrap around her and headed toward the car.

They dined at Bookbinders, the Philadelphia landmark where they had gone on their first date. Janna ate and drank with gusto and left the restaurant invigorated. The next stop was a popular jazz club. Although she enjoyed the music, the cigarette smoke was so thick she asked to leave within an hour. They walked in the night air from Winston's car to his home. Janna, still pleasantly drowsy from the wine they had with dinner, languidly shook the smoke from her hair. Despite her fatigue, she lingered in the bathroom, trying to postpone the moment when she would have to return to Winston. It wasn't that she didn't enjoy being with him, but sometimes she felt she was playing a role that didn't suit her. Tonight that feeling was especially strong. There was a knock at the bathroom door. "You OK in there?"

She opened the door, a hairbrush dangling idly from her hand. "I'll be out in a minute."

He ran his hand through her curtain of hair, revealing ashy shadows beneath the pale blonde exterior. "Your hair is so beautiful. Can't you brush it in front of me?"

"Sure." She slipped her arms through his, allowing his husky body to envelop her slender one. "Thanks for a wonderful evening. I'm sorry I was snippy with you back at the Academy."

"Don't worry about it. As long as nothing is wrong."

"No." She leaned her head against his shoulder. "Nothing is wrong. Nothing at all."

An empty ballroom, all white. And music, the hypnotic, frantic waltz from *Masquerade*. Two men in tuxedos waltz together around and around the circular room with increasing speed. Then the music is gone. The men stop dancing, and begin to kiss passionately.

Janna bolted up in bed and opened her eyes. "Good morning," Winston said brightly, standing in the doorway with a breakfast tray. "I think I finally mastered that French coffee press you gave me." Janna squeezed her eyes shut and opened them again, shaking her head slightly. "Are you OK?" he asked.

She ran her hands over her face, pushing away loose strands of hair. "Yeah. Weird dream, that's all." She grabbed his shirt from the chair and slipped it on.

Winston sat down next to her, setting the tray on her lap. "What was it about?"

Janna took a gulp of coffee. "You know how dreams are. They never make any sense."

Winston stroked her head. "I love the way you look in the morning, like a fairy child."

Janna groaned. "Last night I was all dressed up and you didn't compliment me once. Here I am now, pale as a ghost, hair every which way, and you think this is attractive."

"You looked fabulous last night." His voice betrayed the panic men feel when they've said something wrong to a woman but don't know how to correct it. "I just want you to know I like you this way too."

"Yeah, yeah." She stifled a yawn. "Let's move on to a more interesting topic, like breakfast." She lifted the silver dome, expecting to see something warm and edible. She was flabbergasted when a small black velvet box greeted her instead.

"I was going to give this to you last night, but then I thought it would be more romantic this way." It couldn't be. They had been dating only six months. It was simply a birthday present, she told herself. Earrings, perhaps. She opened the box cautiously, as if something might jump out. "Janna," Winston said, as she stared at the glittering diamond solitaire, "I want to . . ." He faltered. "Will you . . ."

Desperate to stop him, she grabbed his hand and blurted out, "It's too soon." He blinked a few times, stood up, and left the room. "Wait," she said, trying to get out from under the tray. "Winston." She rushed after him into the hall. "It was a beautiful gesture. I'm flattered, really. It's just too soon."

"Right." His face was slack with disappointment.

"Give me another six months. Please."

"Sure," he said flatly. Janna drew him close, feeling as though she had narrowly avoided disaster. Yet she knew six months would make no difference at all.

⌁

Two weeks later, Janna was in the back of her café taking inventory when Elizabeth appeared in the doorway, her teenage face beaming. "There are two really cute guys asking for you."

"They send two guys just to exchange a flat case of ginger ale?" Coming out front, Janna was startled to find Philip and Alex. "This is a nice surprise."

"We were next door at the violin maker's and I remembered this was where you had dropped your key," Philip explained. "Figured you must work here."

"More or less. I own the place."

"I can't believe I've never come in here." Alex peered past her to the desserts in the glass counter. "You're so close to Curtis."

"Please pick out whatever you'd like, my treat."

Alex started to protest, but she silenced him. "Just say 'thank you,' and make sure you don't add 'ma'am.' "

"Thank you, ma'am," they chimed in unison.

Janna placed their pastries and coffee on one of the dozen café tables and pulled up a chair for herself. Alex had barely taken his seat before plunging a huge forkful of chocolate torte into his mouth. "This is amazing," he said as he chewed open-mouthed. He speared another chunk and pushed it into Philip's mouth. After choking briefly on the unexpected offering, Philip made an appreciative murmur. Alex divided the remainder of the cake and placed half on Philip's plate. Philip did the same with his tart.

"I really shouldn't be eating this," Alex said between bites. "Have to watch my weight, you know." He pounded his solar plexus.

Janna examined his reedy frame. "You're a stick."

"A stick that eats like a horse," Philip commented. "Just ask my mom."

Janna looked back and forth between the two of them. "Did I . . . oh, no. You're not brothers, are you?" Janna pressed her hand to the base of her throat, horrified at her mistaken assumption.

They burst out laughing. "Good God, no," Philip said. "He just likes my mother's cooking."

"I'd like *my* mother's cooking too, if she ever did any," Alex commented as he tore open three packets of sugar and dumped them into his coffee.

"You're going to ruin your teeth if you keep that up," Philip scolded, tugging absentmindedly at the unraveling shoulder of Alex's sweater. Alex swatted his hand away.

"Leave me alone."

"Would you look at how he dresses?" Philip shook his head with mock distress.

"He's an artist," Janna said with amusement. "They're allowed some latitude. Anyway, it's cute in a ragtag sort of way." The bell rang and a customer entered. Janna craned her neck to make sure

Elizabeth was at the counter. "So, how long have you two known each other?"

"Since high school." Philip took a small bite of his tart. Janna noticed how delicately he chewed. "I was a senior when we met, so a little more than three years?" He looked to Alex for confirmation.

"You're the math whiz."

"You were high-school sweethearts?" Janna asked with unrestrained delight.

Philip crinkled his eyes. "Are we that obvious?"

"Picking at each other's clothing is usually a dead giveaway."

"I told you not to do that," Alex grumbled.

"Bickering is another," Janna said with an indulgent smile.

Alex leaned toward her, looking intrigued. Her gaze fell on the supple half-moons that swelled below his marble-blue eyes. Although he was not as classically handsome as Philip, the combination of boyish charm and adult sensuality had its own attraction. "I'll have to admit," he said, "I wouldn't have figured you for Dean Feld's wife."

Janna cringed. "I'm not his wife. We've only been dating a few months." She immediately regretted the vehemence of her denial but said nothing to soften it.

More customers came in. "Looks like the late-afternoon rush is under way. I should get back. One of my staff quit yesterday and it's been a little hectic." Janna stood up. "I'm glad you came by. Please stay as long as you like, get refills, seconds, whatever you want. And now that you know how good the food is, I hope you'll come by often."

"Janna," Philip said as she was about to move away. "The person who quit—is that position still open?"

"Yes. Why?"

"I've been looking for a part-time job, maybe ten hours a week. Is that something you'd consider?"

"Sure." She fished in the pocket of her apron for a pen and scrap of paper. "Call me at home tonight and we'll discuss hours and the like. It would be great to have you on board." In truth, she needed another full-time employee. But the boys were entertaining, and that was worth a little inconvenience.

Philip started work the next day. Janna was surprised when he handed her a green card. "You're a citizen of France?"

"I have permanent residency status," he said defensively. "There shouldn't be a problem."

"Oh, there's no problem at all. It's just that you don't have an accent."

"My family moved here when I was a baby. I just haven't gotten around to taking the citizenship test. Too many dead presidents to memorize."

"If my grandparents, who came to this country with no English, could pass the test, then you can."

"Where did they come from?"

She sighed. "Philip, have you noticed the name of this place?" He fumbled. "The Ukrainian Pastry Shop. If you're going to work here, you need to remember it."

"Sorry. I will."

"And don't be shy about throwing around a few French phrases to the customers. People eat that stuff up. You do speak French, don't you?"

"Mais bien sûr."

"That settles it. I'm keeping you at the counter. Between your looks and that accent, I'll have the entire Twelfth Street Gym here every day for cappuccinos."

▲◣◥

Philip was good for business. Traffic, both male and female, increased during the afternoons he worked. A lot of customers flirted with Philip, and some—all men—pushed scraps of paper with their phone numbers across the counter to him. Janna watched with admiration as Philip discreetly tossed each number in the trash the moment the customer stepped away.

Alex always came by at the end of Philip's shift to pick him up. Janna noticed how Philip's working reserve slipped away in Alex's presence, and a different self emerged, warm, comic, infectious. The boys usually lingered, chatting with Janna as Alex stuffed his face with whatever cake or pie was about to go stale. The conversation was light, peppered on the boys' side with witty observations and playful double entendres. It reawakened a carefree, irreverent part of Janna that had long been stifled under a load of adult responsibilities.

A month after he had begun, Philip apologetically told Janna he couldn't continue working because it was taking too much time away from his studies. Janna wasn't surprised. In addition to the burdens of college and the attention required by Alex, Philip seemed to have a fair share of family obligations. He was always coming from, or going to, some younger sibling's school recital, Little League game, or science fair.

Janna was disappointed at the thought of Philip leaving. "I'm going to miss having you around. Alex too."

"We'll still come by," Philip promised. "And we'll see you whenever there's an event at Curtis."

Janna didn't want to wait that long. "I have a better idea. Why don't you guys come over for dinner and sample some Ukrainian specialties I'm thinking of adding to the café menu? We can make it a little going away party for you."

Janna invited them over on a Sunday, so she would have the whole day to cook. When they arrived, the boys tried to follow their noses to the kitchen, but Janna forced them to take the tour first. "On the ground floor there's the laundry room, the garage, and the den." Philip and Alex peaked into a cozy room with bookshelves built into buttermilk-colored walls and a worn burgundy sofa and chairs arranged around a coffee table. They climbed the stairs to the second floor. "The dining room is to the right." She pointed to a long rectangular room with an immense oak table surrounded by a dozen old-fashioned chairs. "And beyond that is the kitchen." She crossed over to the left side of the hall and opened the French doors. "This is the living room."

Philip walked around the large space, which was decorated in serene shades of blue and gray and brightened by a multicolored Oriental carpet. He ran his hand across a Queen Anne settee, an inlaid chess table, and a Tiffany-style desk lamp. "Nice."

Alex walked to the far corner of the room, where a piano sat framed by leafy ferns. He hit a few keys. "Do you play?"

"Occasionally. That was my grandmother's. A lot of this belonged to my grandparents. It was their house before they died."

"They gave you this house?"

"We were very close. I lived here with them for a while." She paused. "Come on, I'll take you upstairs."

"This is the guest room," she said, gesturing to a modest room with a double bed. "Guest bathroom to the left. Then there's my room." She moved down the hall. "On the other side of the floor is another bedroom, but I use it as an office." She suddenly realized she was talking to herself. Backtracking to her room, she found Alex lying spread-eagle on her California king, waving his limbs like he was making a snow angel. Philip was on the other side, bouncing up and down.

"This is the biggest bed I've ever seen," Alex remarked gleefully. "My feet don't hang off the end. And I can toss and turn without bumping into you, Philip."

"I like bumping into you sometimes." Philip fell languidly backward onto the bed. "See you later, Janna." He rolled toward Alex and made a show of air kissing his face.

"Dinner will be on the table in five minutes, with or without you."

"I have no idea what I'm eating, but it's wonderful!" Alex exclaimed.

"Would you like more *vareniki?*"

"Is that the cabbage thing or the dumpling thing? Never mind, I'll take both."

Janna watched them from her grandfather's seat at the head of the table. She found the joy of cooking for others, especially those who ate as heartily as these two, unparalleled. "I guess you're used to the haute cuisine of Philip's mom," she said to Alex. "How does my earthy fare compare?"

"You're asking me to choose between your cooking and that of my *belle-mère?* If Philip doesn't make me sleep on the couch—after he's done with me, of course—his mom will."

Janna laughed and refilled their glasses with the wine they had brought. "So Philip's parents let you stay over?"

"His mom's totally cool." Alex stabbed his fork into a potato pancake smothered in sour cream.

She turned to Philip. "Your dad doesn't mind?"

"He died a few years ago."

"Oh. I'm sorry." She never knew what to say when people told her about the death of a loved one. Traditional expressions of sympathy seemed woefully insufficient. So she did what most people do when the topic arises, she changed the subject. "Anyway, it's nice you and Alex have a place to be together."

"We don't really," Philip said in mild protest. "My room used to be in the basement, which was fine. But it kept flooding, and Alex is allergic to mold. So now we're upstairs. My brother's room is on one side of us, my sisters' on the other. Zero privacy."

"Upstairs or down," Alex declared with a hint of annoyance, "doing it on twin beds pushed together loses its charm after a few years."

"There's always the floor," Philip replied archly.

"Easy for you to say. You're not the one getting rug burns on your—"

"Hello." Janna waved her hand. "There's another person in the room."

"Sorry," Alex said.

"As if the practice rooms at Curtis are more comfortable," Philip continued, oblivious to Janna's entreaty.

"At least they're soundproof." Alex paused, then added, "Well, sort of."

"You guys have sex in the practice rooms?" Janna asked with amusement. "I'd love to see Winston's face if he walked in on that scene."

"Nobody uses those rooms except students," Alex said. "Anyway, you just wedge a music stand under the doorknob and no one can get in."

"That doesn't stop the damn pianists from banging on the door every five minutes and asking, 'Will you switch this room for one without a piano?' "

Alex laughed at Philip's imitation, which was done in a comically high and whiny voice. "I can't help it. I need a piano to compose."

"Compose? Is that what you call what we do in there?"

"Why doesn't one of you get a dorm room or an apartment?" Janna suggested, leaving the table and stepping into the kitchen.

"Curtis doesn't have dorms, and I live too close to Drexel to be eligible," Philip explained. "An apartment would be great, but we can't afford it."

"At least invest in a double bed." Janna returned with coffee and dessert. "Or a futon. They're inexpensive."

"My mom would freak if she saw us dragging a double bed into my room."

"I thought she was OK with you two." Janna saw Alex eyeing the Ukrainsky cake, but she had worked so hard to decorate it that she wanted them to admire it a bit longer before cutting it up.

"She's OK about Alex staying over, but . . ." Philip shifted his eyes. "I've never actually told her he's my boyfriend."

"Your mom's not an idiot, Phil," Alex said with mild reproof. "She must have figured it out by now."

"Even if she has, she's not ready to deal with it. Don't you remember when your parents suggested to her that we might be more than friends? She started speaking in French, pretending she couldn't understand what they were saying."

Janna smiled, remembering how her grandparents used that same trick when it suited them. Noticing Alex's attention was back on the cake, she cut it and passed a large piece to each of them.

"Mmm. Tastes like cognac!" Alex proclaimed, scarfing it down. When he was finished, he brought his napkin to his lips but missed a spot of chocolate cream. "Come here," Philip said and, turning Alex's face toward his, kissed it off. This simple gesture evoked the memory of the dream she had had the night they met. Until this moment, she had not been able to make out the faces of the waltzing men, although she had had little doubt who they were. Now she had none.

Janna had a feeling she would regret what she was about to say but went ahead anyway. "If you're ever really desperate for someplace to be alone together, I have that extra room—" Before she could finish, they jumped up, thanked her effusively, and began clearing the dishes.

"By tomorrow morning you won't even know we were here," Philip promised. "We'll wash the sheets, make up the bed, anything you want."

Janna watched the whirlwind around her with disbelief. She hadn't meant tonight. A moment later they pulled her up out of her chair, crushed her between them in a hug, and bounded up the stairs. Flustered, she sat back at the table, picking off a wool thread that had stuck to her lower lip when it brushed against Philip's sweater. She glanced contemplatively at the thread, then quietly finished her cake.

Later, while loading the dishwasher, Janna was startled by the appearance of Philip in the doorway, dressed only in jeans. She examined the sculpted flesh before her with detachment. He had a young man's body, smooth, lean, and muscular. She couldn't help but compare it to Winston's, even though it was unfair, given the twenty-year age difference between the men. The details of Philip's body were charming—the silky dark hair licking out from the crook between arm and chest, the spray of brown freckles on his shoulders, the ropy blue veins that ran the length of his arms, the flat navel decorated with more soft hair that disappeared into the waist of his jeans. Pretty, yes, but very young and very unavailable.

"Janna, I'm sorry to ask you this, but we didn't expect to be here overnight, and, well," he screwed up his face, "do you have any condoms?"

Janna felt the blood rush to her cheeks. "You've got to be kidding." He gave her a little-boy look. "Upstairs." Philip followed her to her room but stopped respectfully at the door. Janna went into her bathroom and returned with a small foil package. "OK?" She handed it to him, embarrassed and annoyed.

He looked down at it with bewilderment. "I'm going to need more than one."

Janna rolled her eyes. "How many?"

He thought for a moment. "Four?"

"Four?" She was incredulous. "Planning a party?"

He smiled disarmingly. "No, but it's only ten o'clock . . ."

Janna wished she could inspire that kind of passion in a lover, even though the idea of actually doing it four times in one night was far from enticing. Returning from the bathroom, she dropped the additional condoms into his palm. "Listen, Romeo, you'd better make sure each one of these makes its way into the trash, which you will empty into the garbage outside tomorrow morning. Understand?"

He gave her a peck on the cheek. "You're the best."

"Please try not to be too rambunctious. I can't be up all night while you two set a world record."

"Don't worry. We're used to being quiet."

After finishing the dishes, Janna retired to her room to read. This was her favorite place to be, floating in her huge bed, submerged in the underwater colors of lavender and celadon. It was different tonight, though, with them next door. Nice in a way, yet she couldn't help feeling they were taking advantage of her. As she was getting ready for bed, she heard a rhythmic tapping sound, probably the antique headboard making contact with the wall. Great. As she drifted off to sleep, she heard a moan so soft she could caress it with her hand. In her mind she saw the two of them entangled in warm, disordered sheets. She quickly pushed the image away. Go to sleep, she told herself, just go to sleep.

∿∿

Later that week, Philip and Alex showed up at the café, beaming like Cheshire cats. "We don't have classes this afternoon," Philip said, "and were wondering if we could stop by the house."

"I thought you quit working here to have more time to study. What's this, homework for human sexuality class?"

"We're hoping to get an A." The two of them snickered like schoolboys. Janna was amazed at their ability to switch so rapidly from being sophisticated to juvenile.

She disappeared into the back and returned with a key ring, which she dangled over the counter. "Don't break any furniture, OK?"

Philip grabbed the keys. "Thanks."

Janna watched wistfully as they left. "It's so unfair they have to be gay," Elizabeth exclaimed in her pouty schoolgirl voice as she tugged at a piece of hair that had fallen loose from her ponytail. This kind of insidious remark bothered Janna more than blatant slurs. "What a waste" was the most odious, typically uttered by a woman whose looks or personality would have prevented her from having a chance with the spectacular guy in question even if, by some freak of nature, he had been straight. Over the years, Janna had learned to temper her anger at such comments but had never come to understand why her feelings on the subject were so extraordinarily different from those of other women.

The house was quiet that evening when Janna came home, but the backpacks in the foyer announced her guests. Stopping in the downstairs bathroom, she powdered her nose and reapplied her lipstick. She was hyperconscious about her appearance around them, much more so than with Winston. She knew a gay man is far more likely to notice a shiny nose than a straight man, whose interest in a woman's appearance is usually limited to whether she is dressed or naked.

She went into the kitchen to start dinner, then realized she didn't know how many she was feeding. She walked to the foot of the stairs. "Are you two staying for dinner?" A moment later the door to the guest room opened. Alex stuck his head out. Although his body was shielded by the door, Janna glimpsed enough to tell he was naked. She averted her eyes and repeated, "Dinner?"

"Phil, you wanna eat?" Alex called over his shoulder. There was a pause, then, "We'll be right down."

Janna had been concerned there would be some awkwardness during the meal, as she was not used to dining with people who had just emerged from the throes of passion. She also worried the boys might prefer to be alone, and she would feel like an intruder in her own house. Fortunately, her concerns were unfounded. Dinner was relaxed and pleasant. The boys were close and attentive with each other but also drew Janna into their conversations, making her feel welcome and appreciated.

Afterward, Philip and Alex again insisted on clearing the table, but she shooed them away. Dining required a sense of mystery. She would no more allow guests in the kitchen than she would floss her teeth in front of a date. Anyway, she preferred her kitchen as a private sanctuary. Now, ensconced in that sanctuary, a breathtakingly opulent melody reached her, full of anguish and fragile ecstasy. Her eyes followed the path of the music to the living room, where Philip and Alex lay on the couch, kissing quietly. Watching them stirred emotions in Janna that were both confounding and disturbing. They're a beautiful couple, she concluded brusquely, refusing to indulge herself further. It's nothing more than that. She crossed the parquet floor and leaned in the living-room doorway. "What's this?" The boys stopped kissing and looked at her questioningly. "The music."

"Fauré, *Piano Quintet in C Minor,*" Alex said, disengaging himself from Philip. "You like it?"

"Very much."

"It's a present, for you."

"You didn't have to do that."

"Just say 'thank you,' Janna."

Hearing Alex throw back her own words made her smile. "Thank you."

"Do you mind if we make a fire?" Philip asked, getting up.

"Not at all. Sounds romantic." She turned to leave. "When I'm done in the kitchen, I'll be in my office if you need me."

"Is there any way we could stay here again tonight?" Philip blurted out.

"You were at it all afternoon," Janna remarked jovially. "Don't you people ever get tired?"

"It's not that," Alex said earnestly. "We just want to be together."

Janna remembered back to her first relationship, how she'd have to drag herself from her boyfriend's bed after making love when all she wanted to do was cuddle. Maybe her parents couldn't prevent her from having sex, but their restrictions were like a wet blanket on their intimacy. "Sure, you can stay," she said. "And don't worry about stripping the bed. No one else uses that room."

They both thanked her, then Alex asked, with some hesitation, "Are you going to tell Dean Feld about this?"

"No. It's none of his business." She watched the blaze in the fireplace take hold. "Sorry there's no TV down here."

"That's OK." Philip leaned back onto the couch, pulling Alex with him. "We have better things to do."

Janna laughed and shook her head. "Wait till you hit thirty." As she climbed the stairs, she thought, I must be out of my mind.

≈≈≈

In the beginning their visits were sporadic, but before she knew it, they were there all the time. She awoke each morning at six o'clock to the brisk rhythms of Alex's violin. By the time she came downstairs, they were rushing around with toaster waffles and mugs of coffee, eating, dressing, and talking, all at the same time. When she came home in the evening, Philip would be in the den, typing indecipherable equations into his laptop, and Alex would be at the piano, composing. As they no longer could be considered guests, Janna let them help with dinner, relegating them to peripheral tasks even the culinarily impaired could perform. Afterward, as she sipped sherry or Armagnac, the boys would entertain her with amusing anecdotes about their day.

The evenings she spent with them were tough competition for the ones she shared with Winston. Almost three months had passed since his marriage proposal, yet Janna was no more certain of her feelings. It was difficult with Philip and Alex around. They provided a constant reminder of what her relationship with Winston should be, but was not. She envied their flirtatious playfulness, their zestful passion, their easy happiness. Once she saw Philip standing in the bathroom, face covered with foam, waiting patiently as Alex shaved him. She wondered what it would be like to trust someone that much. "Do you always let him do this?" she asked when Alex's razor was a safe distance from Philip's face.

"Just sometimes," responded Philip. "For fun. You should've seen me the first time. I looked like I'd been attacked by a blind barber. But he's improving."

"Good for you, Alex. This way if the music thing doesn't work, you'll always have a day job to fall back on." She wiped a line of shaving cream from Philip's face and flicked it at Alex.

"Surely you realize this means war!" Alex grabbed the can and aimed it at her. Janna stepped back, trying to get out of the line of fire, but wasn't fast enough to avoid being hit. She raced to her room and grabbed a water spritzer. When she returned, the boys were armed with twin cans, and the three of them went wild until Janna was covered in shaving cream and the boys were soaked. She couldn't remember the last time she enjoyed herself so much.

The house resounded with their laughter and youth, and with Alex's vibrant music. Janna felt privileged to be in the company of someone so gifted, let alone have him composing in her home. When he asked her to assist with a chamber piece one day, she was flattered.

"But you play the piano much better than I do," she protested.

"Just enough to compose. Anyway, I'd like to hear it with the violin." He passed her a few sheets of staff paper with his handwritten notations. "Your part is easy." She studied it anxiously. It was not easy. He pulled the piano bench out for her and picked up his violin. "We'll start here." He tapped the page with his bow.

She struggled through the section twice. "I'm sorry I'm having so much trouble. I haven't played for a long time."

"You're doing fine." He made a notation on the sheet music. They went through it once more, then moved on to the next section. Alex stood away from the piano, as he had no need to refer to the score. Each time they stopped, he would lower his arms, leaving the violin jutting out between his chin and shoulder as if it had been grafted there. It made him look like a figure in a surrealistic tableau. Yet he seemed completely comfortable in that stance, so much so that it unnerved Janna, who felt as if she were observing him in some kind of sacred communion with his instrument.

At one point they hit a passage with unusual rhythmic accents that proved especially difficult for Janna. Alex put down his violin, sat beside her on the bench, and demonstrated how the passage should be played. The brush of his arm against hers sent a warm flush through her body, making it hard to concentrate. Still, Janna was able to appreciate the radiant clarity of his rendition. Although embarrassed at her own ineptitude, she continued to assist him that day and in the weeks to come. She was pleased to contribute to Alex's creative process, in however small a way.

≈

A month had passed since the boys had begun staying with her, and Janna was surprised at how well the unusual living arrangements were working. Although she still had disquieting feelings when she saw them kiss or embrace, she was getting used to it. Then, one Sunday afternoon, she was in her closet unpacking from her weekend stay at Winston's. She was startled by the sound of a dresser drawer scraping open directly on the other side of the wall. She froze.

"My parents want me to have dinner with them tomorrow. Want to come?" The voice was faint but sounded like Alex's.

"Like they really want to see my face." This was Philip's voice, so resoundingly clear that Janna almost jumped back from the wall.

"My parents like you," Alex said unconvincingly.

"Your mother barely says two words to me."

"She's like that with everybody."

"And your dad, going on and on about bird-watching, surely the dullest topic on the planet. It's like he's afraid if he stops talking, he'll realize he's sitting down to dinner with the guy who fucks his son." Alex chuckled. The drawer slid shut. "Have you seen my keys?" Philip asked.

"Yeah, they're someplace weird, but I don't remember where."

"Can you give me a hint?"

"Maybe the kitchen. You really should pick a place," Alex gently scolded. "You waste so much time looking for those damn things."

Another drawer opened. "Great advice coming from a guy who once threw his own wallet in the trash can."

"I still can't figure out how that happened." There was a momentary lull. Janna inched closer to the wall. "That shirt looks good on you. Is it new?"

"It's yours, Einstein."

"Really?"

"You have no idea what you own, do you?" Philip asked with amusement.

"Not a clue. That's your department."

"So that's why you keep me around?"

"Come here," Alex demanded playfully, "and I'll show you why I keep you around."

Janna heard footsteps moving away from the wall, then Philip's voice, now as faint as Alex's. "OK, show me." What followed sounded to Janna like tussling, laughter, then silence. Not silence exactly. Kissing, maybe. As the moments passed, Janna realized they were making love. She knew it from the stillness of the room and the barely audible sounds of their bodies touching. Sounds that Janna was imagining more than she was hearing. The joints of the bed began to creak. The stuffy scent of the closet cedar panels was becoming unbearable. Yet Janna remained, her ear pressed to the wall.

"Take it easy," Alex said. "I'm still sore from this morning."

"Don't blame me. That crazy position was your idea."

"You liked it too."

"I like everything with you. You want me to stop?"

There was a pause, then Alex's voice returned, a soft murmur. "Not ever."

Janna was entranced. She wished that she and Winston spoke to each other like that, then realized what she truly desired was far more complicated.

For a long time all Janna heard was a relaxed, rhythmic creaking. She was ready to move away when the sound picked up in volume and rapidity. Two muffled groans followed, a few beats apart. Quiet again. Then Philip's voice, happy and spent. "Wow. That was really . . ."

"Yeah."

"Sorry I made you sore."

"It's OK. It's a good kind of sore. This way, when I'm in class to-morrow, I'll have something to remind me of how good you felt today." Soft laughter. More tussling. "Phil?"

"Uh-huh."

Janna could not make out what Alex said next, but Philip's response was a caressing "Me too." There was a brief hush. "Hey, we'd better get dressed if we want to catch that movie." The footsteps returned, together with the sounds of drawers opening and closing. Philip's voice again, lower. "I think I heard Janna come in awhile ago. You fixed her room, right?" Janna stiffened.

"Yeah, when you went out for your run. Washed the sheets, everything." They were sleeping in her bed? She stepped out of the closet to examine it, first from afar, then up close. Nothing seemed amiss. She pulled back the bedspread. They had fixed it exactly as she did, with the top part of the sheet turned over the blanket. She smelled the pillow cases. Freshly laundered. Other than that, there was no indication they had even been in the room.

The door to the boys' room snapped open, followed by a knock at her door. She opened it to find the two of them with their arms draped loosely over each other. "Hi," said Philip.

"And bye," said Alex.

Janna wished she could confront them about their violation of her trust, but she didn't know how to do so without revealing her violation of their privacy. "See you later," she said, closing the door. She felt a pang of anger at their casual display of affection, then guilt for having such thoughts after listening so intently as they made love.

Janna looked again at her bed. It wasn't surprising they would want to sleep in it when she was gone. It was much bigger than the double in their room, and far more comfortable. Still, the least they could have done was ask. Smoothing a pillow, she told herself no real harm was done. And there was another feeling, a peculiar comfort in knowing they had been in her bed, as if somehow their presence had sanctified it. Stretching out where they had lain, she heard their voices again, distant yet piercingly clear. "You want me to stop?" "Not ever."

After that her closet was a constant temptation. She found one excuse after another to be there when Philip and Alex were in their room. Mostly she heard commonplace conversations about school and family, or the kind of mild bickering all couples engage in. Occasionally, though, she heard faint sounds of lovemaking, sexual banter, or an exchange of endearments, and her heart would beat uncontrollably. Agitated and embarrassed, she would force herself to go across the hall to her office and bury herself in work, but she knew that was only a temporary solution.

When she thought about it later, she realized it was bound to happen. The only question was how and when. It was about two weeks after the closet incident. A pounding headache sent her home from work at midday. By the time she entered the house, the pain was so bad she could barely think of anything other than lying down with an ice pack. Nevertheless, she did remember to check the coatrack in the foyer for Philip and Alex's jackets. Finding nothing there, she assumed the house was empty. She hung up her coat, kicked off her shoes, and walked slowly up the stairs. As she turned on the landing to the third floor, she heard a sound. She looked up and saw the door to the guest room ajar. She stopped and listened for a moment but heard nothing. She could have called out, but she didn't.

She took two more steps up. They were standing against the far wall of the room, kissing, but not tenderly as she had seen them before. These were open-mouthed kisses, passionate, messy, urgent. And they were naked. Janna stood there, unable to move. The silence emanating from the room rendered the scene so dreamlike, she almost doubted the reality of what she was seeing. Neither of them seemed aware of her presence. Philip's back was to her and Alex's eyes were closed, but she knew that could change at any moment. Yet she remained there, hypnotized, as Philip bit Alex's neck in a way that was both delicate and hungry. She watched his tongue, a pink flicker, work its way down Alex's broad, slender chest. Alex's hands rested on the back of Philip's head, both caressing and guiding him. She saw, for the first time, the true strength in those hands. When Philip slipped to his knees, she realized what was about to happen, took two steps backward to the landing, turned, and tiptoed as fast as she could down the stairs.

Her head about to explode, Janna hurried from the house, back to the café. Returning home at her regular time, she opened the door to see the two of them descending the stairs, coats and backpacks in hand. "Hi," she said as calmly as she could. "Heading out?"

"Yeah, we're having dinner at Mom's tonight." Philip slung his backpack over his shoulder.

"She's making coq au vin," Alex said enthusiastically, wrapping his muffler around his neck. In her mind's eye, Janna saw Philip biting that neck. She shuddered. "Are you OK?" Alex asked.

"Yeah. Bad headache, that's all." After they left, Janna crept up the stairs and into their room. She adjusted the door to the angle it had been at when she saw them. Then she walked to where Alex had stood and faced the door. From this position she would have been visible if Alex had opened his eyes. But he must not have, because otherwise surely they would have stopped. She closed her eyes and saw them again, naked, kissing. Opening her eyes with a start, she strode out of the room and pulled the door firmly shut behind her.

◢◣◥

During the next few weeks, memories of what she had seen returned to Janna again and again. The most persistent image was that of Philip kneeling before Alex, which struck her as sexy and sweet. Ironically, Janna would never herself assume that position before a man, finding it demeaning. But it was different when Philip did it, perhaps because he and Alex weren't burdened with thousands of years of inequality. Of course, Janna knew intellectually that she was the equal of her male partners, but on an emotional level she felt insecure. She often doubted herself, whereas most men act as if they know everything, even when they don't.

She wished for that kind of confidence, just as she wished for the
sexual freedom she imagined would exist if men and women were
truly equal.

From the beginning of her friendship with the boys, Janna had
felt herself pulling away from Winston, and it had gotten worse
since she had seen them making love. One night in bed, she
couldn't bring herself to respond to Winston's touch. She felt like
an empty rowboat, adrift in the night sea. Every lighthouse that appeared on the horizon beckoned, but not to her.

"What's the matter?"

"Nothing."

"Janna, you've been like this for weeks." He took a deep breath.
"Are you bored with me?"

"No." She searched for an excuse. "I've just been preoccupied with
work. Everything is set for the expansion of the café, but I'm afraid to
give it the go-ahead. What happens if it's not successful? Then I'll be
stuck with a big mortgage on the house and no way to pay it."

"You have a lot of equity in that house. If there's a problem, you
can always sell it, pay off your loan, and get a smaller place. That
house is too big for you anyway."

"What?!"

"Or you could rent it," he said, nervously backtracking. "Anyway, you have to consider what you want to do with the house if we
get . . . uh, if we decide to live together, or whatever."

Did he really believe she would give up her historic town house
for his bland, suburban rancher? "I'm not selling my house."

"No, of course not." A tense moment passed. "Won't you recon-
sider letting me lend you the money?"

"That's very sweet of you, but no. I'll figure something out." Deciding he deserved another chance, she snuggled up to him. He
kissed her. She kissed back, trying a bit too hard. In the end she
managed to have an orgasm, but it was all release without pleasure,

like a firework that burns a bright line in the night sky, then fizzles and falls quietly to the ground.

"I need to tell you something," Alex said to her a few days later, "and it's not good. I was expecting a call from a friend, so I picked up the phone when it rang."

"Alex, I've asked you not to do that until you hear who it is on the machine."

"I know. Sorry. It sounded like Dean Feld. He asked for you. I said he had the wrong number and hung up. The phone rang a minute later and I let the machine take it."

"Oh, God." She quickly played the message back. Winston's voice sounded calm, as if he'd bought the "wrong number" line. Annoyed, she turned to Alex. "You squeaked by this time, but be more careful."

Shortly after she arrived at his house that evening, Winston asked, "Are you seeing another man?"

"What?"

"I called today. A man answered the phone and said it was the wrong number. I hit the redial button and your machine picked up. What's going on?" He seemed more anxious than angry.

"That was Alex Everett."

"Alex? What was he doing at your house? I thought his, uh, friend doesn't even work for you anymore."

"His name is Philip," she said testily, "and, no, he doesn't work for me anymore, whatever that has to do with it. They drop by the house sometimes, the two of them." She had hoped to stop there, but Winston clearly expected more. "They don't have anyplace to be alone, so I offered—" His eyes widened. "It's not a big deal. They come by when I'm at work. I hardly ever see them."

"How do they get in the house?"

"They have keys."

"They have keys? But I don't even have keys."

"Do you want keys?"

"If I have to ask, there's not much point." He shook his head with disgust. "God, Janna, I can't believe you let them do that in your house."

"They're in love," she answered sharply. "People in love *do that.*"

He laughed. "You are so naive sometimes. It's not about love with homosexuals."

Janna felt her entire body go cold. "You'd better explain that."

"You know what I mean. It's all about sex. Afterward they get up and leave or sleep in separate beds. They're not like us."

"Sleep in separate beds? Where do you get this crap from?" Before he could answer, she grabbed her coat and headed for the door.

"Where are you going?"

"Home."

He looked genuinely confused. "But why?"

"It's over."

"It's what?" he asked with astonishment. "Because of them?"

"No, because of you." As she was about to walk out the door, she stopped. "You know, there was one thing you said that was right. They're *not* like us. I would give my right arm to have their kind of relationship." She slammed the door behind her, confident in her decision, but when she got in the car she dropped her head to the steering wheel and murmured, "Fuck. Fuck. Fuck."

She drove around for a few hours, not yet ready to go home to face the happy couple. She grabbed a burger at a fast-food place, since dinner with Winston had been aborted, but threw away the greasy mess after a few bites. It was almost eleven by the time she pulled into her driveway. She was surprised to see nearly every light in the house on. Stepping through the door, she almost tripped over a full laundry basket left in the foyer. A pizza box was open on the dining room table next to several empty beer bottles. Dishes were piled in the sink. The stereo was blaring The Gipsy Kings. Her Piaf and Callas CDs littered the living-room floor, along with one of her old Bob Dylan cassettes. Bob Dylan? Philip wasn't kidding when he said Alex listened to "everything." A window had been left wide open. Once she closed it, she realized why. The smell was there, faint but distinct. She picked up the ashtray on the coffee table where the remains of the joint lay. Turning away in disgust, she nearly stepped on a tube of lubricant, its midsection bearing the distinctive mark of having been violently squeezed. She walked to the foot of the stairs.

"Philip, Alex, get down here!" There was no response. Listening closely, she heard the shower running. She marched up the stairs and banged on the bathroom door until the water stopped. A moment later they opened the door, holding towels around their wet bodies, looking like young gods emerging from a Roman bath. Their nakedness only fueled her anger. "I've been gone a few hours, and the place looks like a goddamn frat house. I am not your mother, and I am not your maid. I expect you to pick up after yourselves. Understand?" The boys nodded, white-faced and silent. "And I do not appreciate finding little mementos of your undying love for each other around the house. Let me guess, did you do it on my Oriental rug, or my new sofa?"

The boys sheepishly averted their eyes. "Janna, we're sorry," Philip said. "We didn't expect you until tomorrow morning."

"Disappointed you won't be sleeping in my bed?"

Alex looked mortified, but Philip's face was strangely impassive. "Disappointed you won't be watching us?"

"Shit," Alex said in a hushed voice.

Janna felt her throat constrict. "What?"

"Creaky stair. You should get that fixed if you plan to make a habit of spying."

She was shaking with rage. "That was an accident and you know it."

"An accident is five seconds, not thirty."

"Fuck you," Janna said quietly, spinning on her heels and heading toward her bedroom. Then it hit her that he was right. She should have turned around immediately when she saw them that day, but she didn't. She was overcome first by humiliation, then by panic as she realized they would now leave.

She turned back to face them. "I'm sorry. Please don't go."

The boys exchanged a confused look. "Why would we go?"

"Is it our roll?" Alex asked.

"I think so." Philip's head peaked out from behind Alex's where they sat on the living-room floor, interlocked like Chinese pincushions. Alex rolled the dice and moved his backgammon piece to an empty space. "Don't leave that open," Philip warned.

"It's too late." Janna gleefully swept up the dice.

"Next time I want to be your partner," Philip said to Janna. "This one's good for some things." He tugged at Alex's earlobe. "But an expert strategist he isn't."

"Sorry. You two are stuck with each other. For better or worse and all that." Janna rolled, knocked out Alex's piece, and replaced it with one of her own.

"Damn. I knew she'd do that." Philip disengaged himself from Alex. "I'm getting some more wine. Anybody else?"

"Sure, maybe it'll improve our game."

"If that bottle's empty, there's another in the fridge," Janna called after him. A week had passed since their confrontation, and she was relieved to find that everything was more or less back to normal. When she had come down the next morning, the house had been spotless. The boys had apologized profusely for the mess, and she had admitted to having overreacted. No further mention was made of her having stumbled upon them having sex, or them sleeping in her bed. She hoped that meant it was behind them.

Philip returned to the living room with a fresh bottle of wine. Janna was already giddy from the last four glasses but accepted another. "Your guy is in the dungeon." She picked up Alex's piece, waved it over her head, and placed it in a metal ashtray shaped like a pair of Turkish slippers. "And you've got to roll a three to get him out."

"Maybe he wants to stay in the dungeon," Philip said salaciously.

"He could start a group there," Alex exclaimed. "S/M backgammon activists!"

Janna shook her head like a mother amused by the antics of an overactive child. "OK. He's in the dungeon, but the only other person there is Jesse Helms, and he looks real ugly in that leather outfit."

"Oh my God, we have to save him!" Alex rolled a three and a six, getting his piece back in and hitting Janna's open one. "Victory!"

Janna could tell something was wrong with Alex's move, but it took her a moment to figure out what. "You just moved your piece backward."

"No I didn't," he insisted. "You see, I . . ." He looked at the board. "What color am I?"

They all fell into a fit of intoxicated laughter. Janna heard the clock on the mantel strike eleven. "Oh, my movie is on." She leapt up.

"Wait a minute," Alex complained. "You can't leave now that I'm finally getting the hang of it."

"Finish with Philip. He can take my side of the board—that is, if he remembers what color I am." She winked.

"I've had enough." Philip rose, stretching his legs. "What's the movie?"

"Anna Karenina."

"With Garbo?"

"I've never seen that," Alex said.

"You can watch it with me, if you want." Upstairs, Janna sat cross-legged against the headboard and turned on the movie as the boys flopped on the bed. About fifteen minutes into the film, Philip and Alex began horsing around, grabbing and tickling each other. Janna tried to shush them, but to no avail. They started kissing, seemingly oblivious to Janna's presence. She let her eyes linger a bit too long before speaking. "Have we forgotten there's someone else here?" No response. "Don't make me turn the hose on you two."

Philip pulled his mouth away from Alex's. "Janna, be quiet." She froze a moment, then got up and moved toward the door, feeling as though she were in a trance. She hesitated at the threshold, waiting for them to realize how obnoxious they were being. When they still didn't stop, she flipped off the light. As she turned to leave, she heard Philip's disembodied voice behind her. "You don't have to go." Her heart began to pound so hard she thought she was going to be sick. She leaned heavily against the wall, immobilized by fear and desire.

The figures on the bed were illuminated by a soft light that poured in through the window. Janna pretended it was moonlight, although she knew it was her neighbor's flood lamp. Alex was on his back. Philip was kneeling over him, straddling his hips. He pulled off Alex's sweater, then his T-shirt. There was a soft "whoosh" as the cotton escaped from the top of Alex's jeans. I can't do this, Janna thought, but didn't move. Alex unbuttoned Philip's shirt, then, bracing himself up, gently took one of Philip's nipples between his teeth. Philip's eyes were shadowed by the downward tilt of his head, but Janna could see his mouth, open in a small smile. Philip's hands lifted Alex's head to meet his for a series of short, rough kisses, followed by a long, deep one. In the glow of the television, Janna could see Philip reach for Alex's belt buckle. Time to go, Janna told herself, but she didn't. Instead, she sunk to a crouched position on the rug, trying to make herself as small as possible. She was astonished at how aroused she was. But it was more an aesthetic arousal than a sexual one. It was like standing before a canvas by Bonnard, the colors so vibrant, the scene so idyllic, one couldn't help but fantasize stepping into it, leaving everyday existence behind. These lofty sentiments did not, however, explain the hard throbbing of blood in her pelvis. The longer she watched, the stronger it became. It was almost painful. On the television screen Garbo was falling gracefully into a sumptuous chair. Janna wondered why she couldn't be more like her—gorgeous, confident, desired by everyone. Instead, here she was, crouched on the floor, drunk out of her mind, watching two men she adored having sex in her bed.

When she awoke the next morning, her head was aching and her throat parched. But she didn't dare get up, knowing she'd have to face them. She heard Alex tuning his violin, which meant it was very early. She threw a pillow over her head and tried to go back to sleep. Later there were footsteps in the hall. "Let her sleep," Philip said. The footsteps retreated, and after a few minutes, the front door closed. She got up slowly, feeling weak and dizzy. She stripped the sheets methodically, like a hotel maid. When she was done, she looked at the sad, naked bed, slumped to the floor, and began to cry.

Ancient History

From as far back as I can remember, I had problems with the opposite sex. I spent first grade running from a boy who kept lifting my skirt to look at my underpants. The teacher, a nice woman with too many kids to watch, was no help. I finally got him to stop by promising I would take him with me to the seashore the next summer. Every day I told him a new tale of wild sea creatures, of waves that could flip you upside down and umbrellas that flew across the beach like torpedoes on windy days. He loved to hear me tell about the shark scares, how everyone would run out of the water screaming, then stand and watch with fear and delight for the appearance of a silvery fin.

There were lots of games to play at the beach—backgammon and cards for the older kids, building and stomping sand castles for the younger ones. I told the boy about my favorite game, digging a ditch in the sand, covering it with a towel and more sand, then waiting for someone to fall in. We agreed that next summer we would dig a ditch together and lay a trap for my sister. We would have a good laugh when she fell in.

There were some things grown-ups did at the beach that I didn't understand, but I told the boy anyway. Like the old lady in a bikini with leathery skin who'd sit all day by the lifeguard stand like a dog by its master. And the teenage boys who dragged the teenage girls into the water. The girls always screamed "No" but looked like they were having fun. Then there was the time a woman's bathing suit became see-through when she went into the ocean. She looked embarrassed and was trying to hide under the water. My mom ran into the waves with a towel and saved her. All the men around were laughing. The woman told my mom that this was her honeymoon and her husband was one of the laughing men. I felt bad for her, but I didn't say anything because I knew not to interrupt grown-up talk.

In the evenings, after dinner, everyone went to the boardwalk. There were bumper cars, cups and saucers, miniature golf, and a booth with a real fortune teller. Inside the arcades, I watched older kids play pinball. Sometimes my mom would hold me up so I could play too. Every Friday there were fireworks, and the boardwalk was crowded. My dad carried me on his shoulders so I could see better. Afterward, he'd take me to one of the candy stores and buy me fudge, saltwater taffy, or an apple covered with caramel and broken nuts. When we got home, the adults would sit on the porch fanning themselves while my cousins and I lit penny punks and twirled them in the air, making disappearing designs. As we crawled into bed at night we'd hear the bell of the Good Humor man ringing softly as he made his way back home.

I spun my stories, like a tiny Scheherazade, to defend my underpants, and eventually the little boy stopped looking up my skirt. I couldn't wait for the last day of school so I could tell him it was all pretend—that I would never take him to the beach. When the day came, though, I just said my parents wouldn't let me bring anyone. He said he couldn't go anyway. We parted friends, almost.

During most of grammar school, thankfully, the boys were in their girl-hating phase and left me alone. That changed when I was ten. One day after school one of the older boys trapped me in a recessed doorway. I didn't know what he wanted but feared it was something bad. I managed to escape when he was distracted by the sound of adult voices. That same year, my sister Larisa got married. Because she was ten years older than I, our relationship had mostly consisted of my sneaking into her room to play with her clothes and makeup, and Larisa throwing a fit when she caught me. I'd sit at Larisa's vanity table, dousing myself with Jean Naté, draping my neck and wrists in costume jewelry, and modeling Larisa's false eyelashes. I didn't really want to be like my sister, though. Blonde and plump, Larisa hid her intelligence with silly giggles and mindless chatter and spent too much time talking about boys. Although my parents stressed education, finding a Ukrainian husband was equally important. Larisa pursued the latter goal and, once she was engaged, dropped out of college. I thought that was stupid. I liked school, studied hard, and got good grades. When I grew up, I wanted to get a job so I could have my own money and do whatever I pleased. It seemed a lot better than getting married to some bossy man and having babies.

Larisa's wedding was a fancy affair, with almost two hundred people. I was the maid of honor. On the wedding day, Larisa shared her makeup with me, rubbing a stick of rouge on my cheeks. She also showed me how to blot lipstick, file fingernails, and apply eye shadow. I listened, but skeptically. After all, Larisa didn't look like the models in my mom's fashion magazines. Still, it was nice being treated like a grown-up. It gave me the courage to ask about something that had been bothering me.

"Larisa, the girls at school told me something about getting married." Larisa looked up from her dressing table, waiting for me to continue. "They said to have babies the man has to put the thing he pees with inside a hole in the woman that's between where she pees and poops." When Larisa was silent, I smiled triumphantly. "I knew they were lying. There isn't any hole there, anyway. I checked."

"It's true."

I was horror stricken. "But you're getting married! Doesn't that mean you'll have to do it too?!"

"Of course," Larisa said matter-of-factly. "I want children."

"But how could you let that thing touch you? It's dirty and gross!" I was nearly hysterical. "Can't they grow babies in a test tube?"

Larisa laughed. "Janna, stop worrying about what happens when you get married. It's a long time away for you. Anyway, it's not as bad as it sounds." That sickened me into silence. All through the wedding I was plagued by grotesque images. What bothered me the most was that everybody knew what was going to happen to Larisa, but no one was trying to stop it. Instead, people were danc-

ing and laughing and singing. The whole thing was a travesty, a
smoke screen for the disgusting thing that was about to occur. That
day I vowed that I would never let it happen to me. I wouldn't be
tricked by the pretty dress or the presents. I was too smart to be
taken in that easily.

Junior high was a nightmare. I was one of the first girls in my
class to develop breasts and the boys never tired of taunting me.
Looking back, I suppose it was their idea of flirting, but they may as
well have been calling me fat and ugly, because that's how it made
me feel. I avoided the halls and common areas where the guys hung
out and kept my coat on in class. Sometimes I was so overheated I
thought I would pass out. Outside of school was no better. Men
yelled things from cars when I was waiting for the bus or walking
home. Even when I could not hear the words, their mean, angry
voices terrified me.

It seemed like my breasts would never stop growing. It was the
1970s, and large breasts were out of fashion. All of the popular girls
at school, the ones the boys pined over, could double as ironing
boards. One day, as I was helping my mom fold the laundry, I
asked her if there was some way to make my breasts look smaller,
like hers. She snapped the sheet from my hands. "What do you
have to complain about? At this rate you'll have the figure of a burlesque dancer."

A sickening image flashed before my eyes. I was dancing on a
stage with tasseled breasts while men pointed and laughed. "But I
don't want to look like a burlesque dancer. I want to look like a
model."

"Really, Janna," Mom exclaimed with annoyance, "I have more
important things to worry about. There's nothing you can do about
it anyway, so learn to live with it."

I decided to ask the advice of my grandmom the next time I visited her and my grandpop. They lived in downtown Philadelphia,
which everyone referred to as Center City. My baba was an ener-
getic woman, then in her sixties, so small that I towered over her
even at fourteen. When I came over, she was dressed nicely and had

her hair fixed, even though she wasn't expecting me. She always looked good. It was the same with the house. She and my grandpop had filled it with beautiful things, but it was comfortable, too. I loved being there. Sometimes I even fantasized about living there with them. But I couldn't imagine my parents ever letting that happen.

My grandmom sat me down on the couch and offered me every imaginable snack, from fruit to meat pies. When I turned down her offers, Baba sat down next to me, looking concerned. "*Onoochka,* why you don't eat anything? Something must be wrong."

Keeping my voice low so my grandpop wouldn't hear from the other room, I explained my problem. I told her about the boys picking on me, and why. She laughed, but gently. "Most girls, they wish they have this problem."

"Maybe in the old days, Baba, but not anymore. You see these actresses on TV," I gestured to the television set, where a game show played with the volume down. The cohost was a rail-thin peroxide blonde.

My grandmom glanced at the screen, then waved her hand dismissively. "Actresses, what do they know? Look how many times they get married and divorced. I've been married forty years and I can tell you what a man likes. He likes a woman with a nice shape. That's true when I was young, and that's true now. That is why these boys tease you. They think you are beautiful."

"No, Baba."

"Just you wait and see. They are little now, but when they get older, they will ask you to be their girlfriend, and you will spit in their face. Do you understand?"

"*Tak.* But it's not only boys from school. Men in cars say things to me."

Baba looked alarmed. "Stay away from men in cars. They will try to kidnap you." Her voice became very quiet. "Before we moved to Kiev, we live in a village. When I was twelve years old, Russian soldiers come to our town on horses. My father made me hide in our coal bin until they leave. I stayed there two whole weeks. I was so lonely, I would sing to keep myself company, but quietly, so no one would hear. In the beginning, I was mad at my father, but later, I was glad. One of the other girls, Iryna, the soldiers take her away, and we never see her again." I imagined a girl with thick blonde braids and an embroidered peasant dress being snatched off a dirt road by a man on a galloping horse. She screams to her parents, who frantically chase behind, stretching out their arms to reach her, but it's useless. Soon she can no longer see them through the dust. I felt my grandmother squeezing my hand. "I tell your mother to pick you up from school."

"Please don't say anything," I implored. "It will make her angry."

"Then I get your grandfather to pick you up."

"*Neechoho*—it's OK. I'll be careful."

Once I began high school, my breasts finally stopped growing and I noticed some of the other girls catching up. My grandmom was right. The boys who had teased me were now asking me out on dates. But instead of spitting in their faces, I just mumbled, "No, thank you," and slipped away as quickly as possible.

There was one boy who interested me. His name was Brian, and he was the only guy in school who wore an earring. It was in the shape of a lighting bolt—really cool. Everybody said he was a "fag." He sat next to me in Ancient History class. We were assigned to read Margaret Yourcenar's *Memoirs of Hadrian* and Mary Renault's *The King Must Die*. I was astounded to find that both books contained sensuous, if vague, descriptions of love and sex between men. I returned to these passages again and again with guilty fascination. Sometimes in class I would sneak a glance at Brian and fantasize about him doing the things alluded to in the books, things with other guys. At the same time, I wanted to kiss him and be romantic. I knew it didn't make sense, but that was how I felt.

I did kiss him once, at a party. It was my first kiss, but I wasn't sure it counted because he didn't kiss back.

"I'm sorry, but I don't feel that way about you."

"That's OK," I said, the softness of his lips already fading from my memory.

After that he avoided me. I confessed what had happened to a girlfriend. She told me to forget about him, saying, "Homos never change." I didn't know how to explain that I didn't want him to change.

❯❯❯

The following year, I dated a guy at school but broke it off when he got too pushy about sex. Dating a non-Ukrainian, however briefly, was a call to arms to my mother, who began pressing me to attend socials for "young people" at our church. Nothing sufficed as an excuse, not even schoolwork. We had the same discussion over and over.

"It's only Friday," my mom would say, bringing in a dress for me to wear. "You have all weekend to study."

"You could at least let me pick out my clothes," I would counter, fighting for some shred of independence.

"Show me what you're going to wear, then."

I'd put on one of the outfits I had purchased from a funky South Street store with baby-sitting money and timidly model it for my mom. "Oh, Janna," she would say, so clearly disappointed. "What is this? The skirt is so long. You look like an old lady."

"That's the style."

"And the top is too baggy. No one will know you have a nice figure."

"Am I supposed to be on display?"

"What was wrong with the dress I chose for you?"

"It's not me, Mom."

My mother would give me a look that instilled both guilt and fear. "I ask you to do one thing for me . . ."

So I would go to the dances, in the dresses my mother picked out, but never step onto the dance floor. I just wasn't attracted to Ukrainian guys. Their physical appearance was too Old World, even the ones who were second generation, like me. The first time I went to a dance I spent the entire evening circling the outside of the church, daydreaming and looking at my watch. After that I hid a book in my purse and would sneak off to one of the Sunday-school rooms to read until it was time to go. The drive home with my mom was the worst part of the evening.

"So, did you meet any nice boys?" she would ask in a giddy voice, as though we were girlfriends swapping stories about our big night out.

"I told you, only losers go to these things."

"You'll never meet anyone with that attitude. There might be a guy there who didn't want to come either. Maybe you'll have something in common."

"I don't have anything in common with these people."

"How can you say that? You share the same heritage."

"That's not enough."

"You are so negative, Janna. You don't realize how lucky you are. Your father and I work very hard . . ." I would tune out, counting the minutes until we were home and I could disappear into the refuge of my room.

Things reached a boiling point during my senior year, after a dinner party at our house. Everybody there was family except one man, a distant cousin of my aunt's husband. He was a lawyer, in his late twenties, pompous, boring, and overweight, with a big bushy mustache and thinning hair. At first, I couldn't figure out why he'd been invited. I became suspicious when my mother seated him next to me at the table, but the possibility was too awful to consider. After everyone left, and I was helping my mom clean up, she asked, "What did you think of Pavlo?"

"Who?"

"Your uncle's cousin."

I wiped the table. "Kind of creepy."

"He seemed to like you," she said cheerfully as she loaded the dishwasher. "Would you consider going out with him?"

"You've got to be kidding. He's gross."

"I thought he was quite charming."

"Then you go out with him."

"Don't take that tone with me. One date wouldn't kill you."

"If he comes here, I swear I'll lock myself in my room, like Baba did when her parents tried to make her marry that man with gold teeth."

My mother sighed. "You pay too much attention to your grandmother's crazy stories."

"I'm not going out with him."

"Fine," she said tightly. "Do whatever you want."

I wondered what image my mom had of me that she would try to fix me up with a man like that. I wished I could chalk it up to Mom's bad taste in men, but that wasn't it. My dad was good-looking, smart, and the life of the party. Why would my mother think I'd settle for so much less?

The more strained my relationship with my mom became, the more I looked forward to spending time with my grandparents. In addition to visiting them every Sunday with the rest of the family, I stopped by once a week for a piano lesson with Baba, something I had done since I was a child. Baba had trained in Kiev with a famous teacher, but she never played professionally. "Back then, a woman studies piano to show she is from high-class family, not for career. My teacher said I was the best student, and if I was a man, I could make money giving concerts. But it would not look right for a woman to do that. So, I play for myself, and I teach. It was not so bad. But is better now. Woman can do anything she wants. You can do anything you want!"

After my lesson, Baba would play her favorite classical recordings. Although the records were old, some of them 78s, I could still hear the beauty of the music through the scratched vinyl. If we listened to an opera, Baba would relate the story as it went along and, during the most dramatic parts, act out the roles. My favorite was *Tosca*. I loved watching Grandmom in the title role, stabbing the air with an imaginary knife to fend off the advances of the evil

Scarpia, as the soprano sang, "Questo è il bacio di Tosca!" This is the kiss of Tosca.

I also enjoyed spending time with my grandpop, my dido, who was a quiet man, with the same good looks as my dad. He had been a successful restaurateur and chef before his retirement. He taught me secrets of European and Ukrainian cooking, and his specialty, pastry making. Soon I was creating replicas of his cakes, pies, and delicate confections. Dido encouraged me to apply to professional cooking school. But my parents wanted me to get a business degree, and for once I agreed with them. I wanted to keep my options open, and a business major seemed a practical choice.

Like my parents, my grandparents expected me to marry a Ukrainian but accepted the excuse that I didn't want to get serious with anyone until I had settled into a career. The truth was that I daydreamed constantly about having a boyfriend, but none of the guys I met came close to my romantic ideal.

Shortly after graduating from high school, I attended a party for a classmate. The classmate's brother was there, home from college for the summer. Although Scott was an average-looking guy, I was impressed by his gentleness and humor. We went out a few times, but always on the sly, so my parents wouldn't find out. Then Baba broke her hip and was bedridden. I volunteered to move into my grandparents' house to care for her. Although I had a lot of responsibility during the day, I was able to slip out in the evenings to see Scott. Before things went too far, I told him I was a virgin and wanted to go slow. He respected my wishes. Looking back, I realize what a gentleman he was, keeping his clothes on as he made love to me with his mouth. Now when I think about it, I laugh at how innocent I was, confounded that first time by the peculiar feeling of my legs drifting away from my body. It was only afterward when I realized I had had an orgasm.

We did not engage in intercourse until the end of the summer. He offered to use a condom, but I had heard they weren't foolproof, and pregnancy was a terrifying prospect. The pill seemed the safest bet. The only place I knew to go was Planned Parenthood. I had never been to a gynecologist before. For some reason I assumed the doctor would be a woman. When a man walked into the examining room, I panicked but was too embarrassed to ask for a female doctor. The examination was painful and unpleasant. After having a piece of metal shoved up inside me without warning, the first time with Scott wasn't that bad. Eventually I came to enjoy it, mostly because it made me feel close to him. The possibility of having an orgasm this way, though, seemed preposterous.

Now, reflecting back on the relationship, I'm glad Scott was the first. He was an unselfish lover and made me feel comfortable about my body, assuring me over and over that I was beautiful. It was something I desperately needed to hear, even if I did not dare to believe it.

At the end of the summer, Scott returned to college in Boston, and I began attending the University of Pennsylvania. It was the fall of 1978, and it was a very lonely time for me. Scott and I spoke regularly, but I saw him only once before the winter break. He invited me to Boston, but I knew my parents wouldn't allow it. To make matters worse, I was one of a very small minority of undergraduates who commuted. Among Ukrainians, it was standard for children, especially girls, to live with their families until marriage. My sister had done it, and I was expected to do the same. I managed to negotiate a deal with my parents to stay in Center City with Baba and Dido during the week, which made my commute fifteen minutes instead of an hour, and return home on the weekends. Although this arrangement was preferable to staying at home, it didn't help me make any friends. Almost all the socializing at the university took place in the dorms. Lunch was an especially difficult time. Freshmen ate in the student cafeteria, which I couldn't do because I didn't have a meal card. Every day I sat in an empty salad bar off campus, my sole lunch companions Colette, Balzac, and Mishima.

When Scott came home at Christmas, I noticed his manner had changed. When I asked what was wrong, at first he said, "Nothing," but then confessed, "It's hard with you here and me up in Boston. I'm not sure this is really working."

"Are you saying you want to break up with me?"

He looked guilty. "I guess so."

I was hurt, but deep I down knew it was for the best. It didn't make a lot of sense to have a relationship with someone you hardly ever saw. What I missed the most was his friendship. Although I had developed a few casual acquaintances at school, I was still miserably lonely. In the middle of my second semester, I was seriously considering dropping out. When I told my parents, they quickly retreated from their previous position and gave me permission to move on campus in the fall. There were two provisos. I had to spend every other weekend at home and join the family for dinner every Sunday at my grandparents'. I readily accepted, planning to reduce my visits home to once a month as soon as possible. Visiting my grandparents was different. I hated to disappoint them and kept Sunday dinner sacrosanct.

I was so excited about living on campus that I had everything packed by the middle of the summer. Moving day was frantic, vying with so many other students for the elevator, then trying to cram everything into a space the size of a sewing room. My roommate was an emaciated and uncommunicative girl from someplace called Long Island. She had gotten to the room before me and taken the better mattress and less wobbly dresser. I didn't care. All that mattered was being on campus. After unpacking, I went to the student lounge, where people were gossiping about a guy on our floor who was painting his room pink. They spoke as if it were a major scandal. Curious, I wandered along the hall until I saw a door half open to a shocking-pink wall. Inside was a pixieish young man with fine blond hair, standing on a folding chair and hanging a pink Japanese lantern over a bare bulb.

I stuck my head in the door. "Great color."

He turned and smiled. "Spicy pink. A dollar ninety-eight a gallon. I can get you some if you'd like." I detected a slight Southern accent.

"I thought we weren't allowed to paint our dorm rooms."

"You must be a freshman," he said wryly, stepping down from the chair and waving me in.

"Sophomore, but I just moved on campus."

"We must have a tête-à-tête so I can fill you in on the real rules around here. Right now, though, I'm expecting guests. Would you like to join us for tea?"

I looked around the small room, which barely held the single bed, dresser, desk, and minirefrigerator. "I don't want to crowd anyone."

"Don't be silly." He threw a few decorative pillows onto the bed, then, like a magician, pulled swatches of colorful fabric out of a box and draped them over two chairs. As a final touch, he hung a vintage theatre poster advertising Oscar Wilde's *Salome*. The ordinary room now looked almost exotic. "Wouldn't this make a great opium den?" he asked excitedly. "Although I suppose the walls would have to be a darker, more decadent shade." He surveyed the walls pensively, a finger to his lips. "Blood red, perhaps." There was a knock at the open door.

"I hope we're interrupting something," a man said as he entered, but when he saw me he added sourly, "Oh, I guess not." Another young man followed. They both gave the host an affectionate, though perfunctory, kiss on the lips. It startled me. I had never seen men kiss before, except of course in my imagination.

"I'd introduce this charming lady to you," my host said to his friends, "but she has neglected to tell me her name."

"Janna."

"*Enchanté.*" He bowed and kissed my hand. "I'm Denton, and these two young rogues are Ian and Arthur."

"Hi," said the one named Ian, smiling as he shook my hand. Arthur, the one who had made the comment about interrupting us, mumbled a hello, dropped into one of the chairs, and lit a cigarette. Denton graciously offered us tea from an heirloom set. Everyone accepted but Arthur, who waved the styrofoam cup he had brought with him by way of explanation.

As the outsider in the group, I said little but listened closely. From their conversation, I could tell they were all sophomores, like me, and had been friends since their freshman year. Denton, an architecture major, was from Savannah and, it seemed, well-heeled. Ian, a local boy of Irish descent, was studying art history. He appeared shy at first, but when the three began to relate stories of their summer exploits, his tales easily rivaled those of the other two. Arthur was a scholarship student from a large farming family in the Midwest. A German major, he was astute, arrogant, and mean-spirited. Yet, of the three, he was the most intriguing. He didn't say anything to me until late in the visit, when, with an abruptness I later learned was habitual, he asked, "So, you a dyke?"

"No," I answered cautiously.

"Then you're a fag hag."

"Excuse me?" It was the first time I had heard this term, and I didn't like it.

"You do know we're gay, don't you?"

"No!" I exclaimed with feigned surprise. "And I thought Ian was referring to his girlfriend in that quaint story he told about getting screwed on top of a bar."

For the first time that afternoon, Arthur cracked a smile. Then he stood up, crushed his empty coffee cup and threw it across the room into the trash. Stepping out the door, he turned to Denton. "Bring her along next time."

When I returned to my room later that afternoon, I was bursting with excitement. My first day there and already I had made friends, among gay men no less. Better yet, I was not attracted to any of them, a definite plus if I wanted to avoid a repetition of what had happened with Brian in high school. Denton and Ian were too effeminate for my taste, although "affected" seemed a more accurate description, as I had never seen a woman act like that. Arthur was affected in a different way, with his "portrait of the artist as a young Trotskyite" look, complete with wire-rimmed glasses, uncombed hair, and disheveled army-navy attire, all cloaked in the stink of stale cigarettes and burnt coffee. As cantankerous as he was, and as silly as the other two were, I had enjoyed being with them and hoped they would open their circle to include me.

The next day Denton invited me to join them for lunch at an off-campus diner. It was a dingy place of questionable cleanliness. The guys were already seated at a table when I came in. I could hear Arthur's voice booming across the room, "And then the guy has the nerve to call me 'bourgeois in bed.' Can you believe it? I showed him a thing or two. By the time I left he could barely walk."

"How chivalrous of you," Denton quipped.

"More to the point, how proletariat," Ian said.

I sat down. "Just in time," Denton said. "Arthur was relating a very amusing story."

"I heard," I responded dryly, "along with everyone else in the place."

"Well, what do you think?" Arthur's eyes shone maliciously behind his tiny frames.

He was baiting me. I knew I had to come up with something marginally witty. "What I think is, I wish you were a little more bourgeois in your culinary tastes." This garnered a slight chuckle from them, sufficient to pass Arthur's test. "Seriously," I continued, "there's another diner a block from here. Same food, same prices, much better decor."

"We rather like the decor here," replied Denton. I followed his gaze to a busboy clearing tables, a nondescript man in his midtwenties.

"What's so special about him?"

"Isn't it obvious?"

I didn't get it, but remained silent, not wanting to appear stupid. As the man got closer to their table, the guys' comments became bolder. "No," said Ian, shaking his head sadly, "I'm afraid I couldn't do it. He's simply too big."

"Are you kidding? You'd amputate one of your legs if you had to," Arthur retorted.

Ian laughed. "I would, wouldn't I?"

Finally, I realized what they were talking about. "Don't you guys think of anything else?"

"But what could be more important?" Denton cried with a gasp. "How about getting a decent meal?"

Despite my qualms, I met with them almost every day in that dive. I also spent a lot of time in Denton's room, in part because I enjoyed his company, in part to get away from my bulimic room-mate. Denton occasionally mentioned going clubbing with Ian and Arthur. I hoped they would invite me along, and eventually they did. In preparation, I ran up my dad's "for emergencies only" credit card in the trendiest store in town, buying black leather jeans, a motorcycle jacket, and boots. To complete the outfit, I picked up a package of men's undershirts and tore off the sleeves and collar, copying Ian's signature look. At the appointed date and time, I met the gang at Arthur's room for what was supposed to be drinks, but which I suspected was an inspection. Denton, who was already drunk, grabbed me and shrieked, "Your lipstick matches the color of my wall! Give it to me. I want to see if it glows in the dark."

Reluctantly, I pulled the lipstick from one of the zippered pockets of my jacket. "It doesn't glow in the dark."

"Chanel, my favorite." He went to the mirror and applied the fuchsia color to his lips.

"Slow down, that's expensive," I chided. Denton hit the lights. "I told you it wouldn't glow in the dark." Denton turned the lights back on and cleaned off the lipstick.

"Who cares about lipstick. It's the leather I want, baby!" Ian exclaimed as he ran his hand down the back of my jacket. A small, sensual shiver coursed through my spine, surprising and confusing me. "If you were a man," Ian continued, "you could have me anytime."

"Anyone can have you anytime," Arthur retorted. "It's too bad Janna isn't a man, though. Dressed like that, she could get us in anywhere. As it is, we'll have to rely on Denton's wiles."

"I could put my hair up in a cap," I offered.

"Don't be ridiculous. You'd never pass as a man." This disappointed me, although I couldn't say why. "The reason this fetish gear looks good on you is because you're so feminine. It provides an interesting contrast. Here." Arthur took a studded dog collar from his dresser and wrapped it around my wrist. "A loan, not a gift."

As we approached the club, I pulled out some money. Denton pushed my hand down roughly. "We never pay to get in clubs," he admonished. Embarrassed, I tucked the money away and, after that, timidly followed Denton's lead. He approached the doorman, batting his eyelashes and wagging his little ass. We were ushered in without a glance toward the ticket window. I tensely followed the guys through a winding narrow hall. Each man who passed seemed to glare, making me feel like an unwelcome guest. When we entered the main part of the club, I was relieved to see a few other women. Still, the experience was intimidating. That feeling never changed, no matter how often I went to gay clubs. But the rest of the atmosphere more than made up for it. The sexual energy was incredible. Men cruising men, men dancing with men, men touching men. And in a dark corner, two men kissing like fugitives in an open city. It was astonishing to be surrounded by such rampant male sexuality, yet feel completely unthreatened, something that would be impossible in a heterosexual setting.

When I got back to my dorm that morning, at three o'clock, I lay in bed, too geared up to sleep. For the first time I consciously admitted that I liked this, watching men together. It gave me a warm, excited feeling. I wondered if all women felt this way but were afraid to acknowledge it. That seemed unlikely. Yet it was also hard to believe I was the only one. I was fairly certain Yourcenar and Renault shared this same trait, since they had written so eloquently about gay male love. That both of these authors were lesbians, however, was perplexing. I assumed my own interest in gay men was based in heterosexuality. I liked beautiful men, so it made sense that I liked to see them together. But maybe it was something else entirely. Perhaps my attraction grew out of early bad experiences with straight men. These experiences, though, surely paled in comparison to those of many women who did not share my predilection.

Even if this sexual quirk was present only in a minority of women, why was it so completely ignored? Was it because any form of female sexuality not revolving around heterosexual men was deemed aberrant or, worse, inconsequential? The silence on the subject was especially galling given that the corresponding phenomenon, straight men being aroused by lesbian sex—or faux lesbian sex—was discussed ad nauseam.

Once, in my twenties, I was with a female friend in a neighborhood bar. An obnoxious man approached us and wouldn't go away. Hoping to discourage him, I said we were lesbians. He immediately suggested a threesome. I marveled at his temerity. "I have a better idea," I said in a seductive voice. "See that man over there?" I pointed out a burly stranger. "I'd love to watch him fuck you." He turned and ran out so fast you'd have thought the other guy had whipped it out and was greasing up.

Although we had a good laugh over it, my friend was clearly uncomfortable. "I'm glad you got rid of that guy, but what you said to him was really disgusting. Not the lesbian part. I understand why you said that. But watching two men do it? Ugh! How could you think of something so horrible?"

It was then that I realized how threatening my sexuality could be to others. Here was my friend, an intelligent, college-educated woman, who would prefer to be stuck with a creep all night than to consider, even for a moment, the idea of two men having sex. I was tempted to tell her that I wouldn't have put those two guys together anyway—they were clearly wrong for each other. Truth, however, was seldom the best defense.

As my sophomore year progressed, I made a few new friends but spent most of my time with the triumvirate. Although they were generally open with me, there were certain aspects of their lives they didn't share. They constantly boasted of their sexual exploits, usually in lurid detail, but were silent on the subject of boyfriends and relationships. I was sure none of them was involved with any of the others, although I picked up that Arthur and Ian had had some kind of fling last year. Arthur was downright hostile to emotional attachments, calling them a waste of time and against men's nature. I liked to think this was a lame attempt to hide some gut-wrenching love, although certainly not for Ian. While comely, Ian seemed too vacuous to be anyone's love interest. He was also a tremendous slut. I hate to use that word, but it fit. Whenever we went to a bar or club he quickly disappeared, not to be seen again until the next day, when he regaled us with stories of his escapades. Denton, on the other hand, always made it a point to accompany me back to our dorm. Frequently, though, he dropped me off and retreated back into the night. Although he was more reserved about broadcasting the details of his sex life, I suspected it differed from Ian's only in quantity, not in its nature.

The boys occasionally went to New York, the main purpose of which seemed to be visiting sex clubs. That they didn't invite me was hardly surprising. Even if these places admitted women, which was doubtful, I never would have gone. Nevertheless, I found it rude that they made inside jokes about the trips in my presence, as if to remind me that I was "one of the boys" only to a point.

There were other problems with spending all my time with gay men. When in public, I had to listen to them gush over every marginally attractive man who happened by. Intelligent discussion was impossible, especially with Denton. No matter what I said, he would respond, "That's good," never taking his eyes off the passing parade. I began to feel extraneous, not to mention undesirable, simply by virtue of being female.

Things took a turn for the better during the second semester of sophomore year. I was sitting on the library steps with Denton and Ian when a male student approached. He was blond and green eyed, with handsome features and an athletic, if somewhat stocky, build. The boys were ogling him and exchanging whispered comments when, to everyone's surprise, the guy stopped in front of us. "Excuse me. Don't you take Financial Accounting with Professor Quinn?"

I looked to Denton and Ian, assuming the man was addressing one of them. After more than a semester hanging around gay bars, I wasn't accustomed to being the recipient of male attention—positive male attention, anyway. Then I realized Denton and Ian would sooner join a rodeo than take an accounting class. "Yes," I answered. "I'm in that class."

"I'm Nate." He stretched out his hand. I shook it and introduced myself. "The thing is, I missed class last week and was wondering if I could copy your notes." I pulled out my notebook and tore out a few sheets. "Thanks a lot." He flashed a winning smile, then dashed into the library. When he was out of sight, Denton and Ian started shrieking and pulling on my arms.

"Look what our little vixen caught today!" Denton exclaimed.

"Will you lend him out to us, please?" Ian begged.

"Oh, for God's sake." Irritated, I pulled my arms free. "He only asked for my notes."

"No way, honey. He's hot for you," Denton insisted. "But you'd better play your cards right. Don't jump into bed with him right away."

I looked at him peevishly. "I'm not you."

A few minutes later, Nate emerged from the library. "Here he comes," said Ian excitedly. *"Sois sage, sois chic."*

Denton grabbed Ian's shoulder. "Oh, my God, the boy can read! And James Baldwin no less."

"Baldwin who? I read that in a bathroom stall while some guy was giving me a blow job."

"Shut up!" I hissed before turning a smiling face to Nate.

"Thanks," Nate said, returning the notes. "You heading to class?"

Nate and I dated for most of the semester. I saw the guys less because of it but still met with them occasionally for lunch. I especially missed our jaunts to local clubs, but that time was now reserved for Nate. Some evenings, though, walking with Nate, I could see the pink light from Denton's room glowing across campus, a gay beacon in the night. It made me wish, if only for a moment, that I were single again. Ironically, being with Nate seemed to increase my stature with the boys. They begged for details about his body and sexual performance, but I didn't take the bait. In truth, he was a bulldozer in bed. I never came close to an orgasm, which wasn't surprising since he didn't do anything that could lead me to one. But I wasn't confident enough to make suggestions, and he didn't seem the type who would be receptive to them. Still, I was relatively happy with the relationship. It was nice being the center of attention for once.

My feelings about Nate changed during campus "Gay Day." Students were supposed to show support for gay rights by wearing blue jeans. As jeans were virtually the school uniform, the idea was to inconvenience those who were small-minded. It was the first time I had seen Nate in corduroys. When I asked about it, he said he didn't want people to think he was a "faggot."

I was infuriated. "It doesn't mean you're gay, just that you support gay rights."

"Who else would support it?"

I gestured to the jeans I was wearing.

"You don't count," he said dismissively. "You're a girl."

"And you're an asshole." I stomped away, wondering if I was ever going to count to anybody.

As troubling as this exchange had been, I was more disturbed by the guys' reaction. "So what?" Denton said.

"But he used the word 'faggot' to my face," I protested. "And he knows I have gay friends."

"He's so hot, honey," Ian said, "if he'd fuck me, I'd let him call me anything he wants."

Disgusted, I looked to Arthur. "Why are you asking these whores?" He took a drag on an unfiltered cigarette. "Unlike them, you have principles, and," he glanced coldly at Ian, "self-respect. If the guy's attitude bugs you, dump him. You're a beautiful woman. You can have anyone you want."

I thought a lot about what Arthur said, dwelling the most on his off-handed compliment at the end. To be called beautiful by Arthur, who had not one iota of interest in women, was the most flattering thing I could imagine. It gave me the confidence I needed to break it off with Nate.

◆◆◆

Junior year started promisingly. I was assigned to a room in the same dorm as Denton again, and this time I snagged a single. Two weeks into the semester I met Marcelo in my Commercial Banking class. Even in the large auditorium, he stood out, a tall, fragile boy on crutches. Especially intriguing was the faded T-shirt he wore, bearing the logo *Lycée Français de Vienne*. Thinking he might be gay, and possible boyfriend material for one of the guys, I grabbed a seat in his row. When the class broke, I noticed he was having trouble gathering his things.

"Need some help?"

"Thank you."

I lifted his backpack for him. "What happened to your leg?"

"I fell off a bicycle. Clumsy, no?"

There was nothing clumsy about him. I tried to place the accent. "So, you've lived in Vienna?"

"But how did you know?" he asked with genuine astonishment. I gestured to his shirt. "Ah, yes." Students from the next class began filing in. We exited slowly into the hall.

"I'm trying to figure out if you're Austrian or French."

"I am Argentine." From his physical characteristics, I never would have guessed he was from South America. His skin was as pale as an Englishman's. His hair was light brown on his head, nearly transparent on his arms, and peach fuzz on his face. The only trait in line with his origins were his warm, dark eyes.

"How did you end up with a T-shirt from a French school in Vienna?"

"It is complicated. We lived in Buenos Aires until I was thirteen. Then my father became ambassador to Austria, and we moved to Vienna. I knew no German, but I did know French, and there was a

French lycée in Vienna. So that's where I went to school." He stopped when we reached the elevator. "Now you know everything about me, and I, I do not even know your name."

"Janna."

"That is a beautiful name. I am Marcelo." He pronounced it with a soft "c." He extended his hand as graciously as the crutches would allow. "I am sorry to go, but I have another class, and already I am late. We will see each other next week, no?"

"I'll look for the crutches."

"By then they will be gone. Look for my face. I will be the guy with the biggest smile."

Walking away, I decided my initial assessment had been wrong. Marcelo was not gay. He certainly had a quality about him, though. Some people would call him androgynous, but to me that term signified someone who was sexless, and Marcelo was anything but that. He had the same boyish quality I would later find so attractive in Alex, except that Marcelo was a refined European boy, whereas Alex was a decidedly unrefined American one.

After our next class, Marcelo asked if I wanted to see *Cabaret*, which was playing at a nearby revival theater. We ate at a casual, noisy restaurant before the film. When the check came he grabbed it.

"I want to split it," I said.

"It is not necessary. You want me to know you are an independent person, and already I know this."

"Marcelo, hand it over." I stretched my hand out, palm up, across the table.

He hesitated, then reluctantly turned over the bill. "See, already I cannot resist you. We split it, but next time—"

"We split it again."

"I do whatever you say." He spread his arms open, as if conceding defeat, but with a big grin. "You are the boss."

After the movie we walked to Marcelo's West Philadelphia apartment. It was the nicest student apartment I had ever seen. Framed movie posters decorated the walls. Books in Spanish, French, German, and English filled the shelves. There was an extensive entertainment center, and real furniture. We sat on the floor, against the couch, discussing the movie. I don't know who initiated the first kiss, but it hardly mattered. His mouth was sweet and soft. I was amazed at how quickly and deeply he aroused me, much more so than Nate, whose perfunctory kisses were solely a means to an end.

After we had been kissing awhile, I slipped my hand under his T-shirt and caressed his thin, hairless chest. When he reached gently under my top, I pulled back. "I'm sorry. I'm not ready for that yet."

"OK," he said amiably, withdrawing his hand.

"I know it's not fair. I touched you."

"It does not matter. When you are ready, you will tell me." He kissed my fingertips. "Anyway, it is better to wait, no? It creates intrigue." He laughed, kissed me some more, then walked me back to my dorm.

Before things went any further, I decided Marcelo would have to pass the litmus test—meeting the terrible threesome. I begged the guys to behave themselves. To my relief, they were polite and said nothing the least bit obscene during our lunch together. Arthur even conversed briefly with Marcelo in German. Afterward, as Marcelo and I walked across campus, I asked him what he thought. "They seemed very nice. And the one with the glasses speaks excellent German."

"Does it bother you that I spend so much time around gay men?"

He hooked his arm through mine. "But there is no one I would rather you spend time with. I do not have to worry about them trying to steal you away from me. So it is for the best in this best of all possible worlds!"

I met with the guys later that afternoon on the library steps. "What do you think?"

There was silence. Eventually Denton spoke up. "I liked the jock better."

I groaned. "He was a pig."

"But a sexy pig," Ian chirped.

"You don't think Marcelo is sexy?" Denton and Ian were silent. "Arthur?"

"He's kind of cute for that type. A little too tall, but I could go for him in a pinch." Arthur let his cigarette ash drop on the stone step. "You did good this time, Janna."

"Thanks."

Arthur's expression remained impassive. "Don't mention it."

I forced myself to wait another two weeks before sleeping with Marcelo, to make sure there weren't any unpleasant aspects of his personality waiting to reveal themselves. I was delighted to discover that he was everything he appeared to be. Making love with him was utterly different from anything I had experienced before— more sensuous, more erotic. I had an orgasm every time. The only problem was intercourse. He was simply too big. It was beyond me why Denton and Ian thought it was a good thing for this part of the male anatomy to be so hypertrophied. Maybe they were built like the Holland Tunnel. I was not. I tried my best to bear the discomfort stoically, but after our third time together, Marcelo asked, "What is the matter?"

"Nothing."

"Did I hurt you?"

I waited a little too long before responding. "No."

He looked in my eyes. "Please tell me."

I hesitated again. "A little."

"Is this every time?" I nodded cautiously. "But why did you not tell me?"

"I was afraid you wouldn't want to see me again."

He propped himself up on his elbow, his brow furrowed. "How could you think that of me?"

"I'm sorry. Don't be angry."

"No, no," he said, lying back down and taking me in his arms. "I am not angry. And it is I who should be sorry, not you."

"I'll get used to it. It'll just take some time."

"It makes no difference to me how we make love. There are many ways. I let you choose."

Despite these heartfelt assurances, I made sure we engaged in intercourse at least once a week, afraid he would lose interest in me otherwise. Although he was as gentle as possible, the activity was never more than barely tolerable for me. It was especially frustrating because, when I felt his body next to mine, I ardently desired intercourse. Once we started, though, it felt nothing at all like what I had craved. That had been true with my other boyfriends, but the problem there had been the dulling of sensation. With Marcelo I felt things, but they were all unpleasant, the worst being the disturbing sensation that I was going to lose control of my bowels. It was as if my body used a siren song to lure me into an activity designed to get me pregnant, then withdrew all pleasure once I got too close to the rocks to pull away.

We did make love other ways. My favorite was straddling his hips and rubbing myself against him until he came. It almost seemed like I could come this way too, but ultimately I needed more. On other occasions I used my hands or mouth to bring him to climax, the latter being no easy feat given his size.

One morning, I came into Marcelo's kitchen to find him juggling fruit. "That's pretty good," I said, pouring cereal into a bowl. He tossed me an apple. "Can I have some of that banana?"

"No," he said, flopping down on one of the kitchen chairs. "This is for demonstration purposes only." Then, amid much flourish, he began to fellate it.

I laughed heartily. "Is that supposed to be me?" He nodded as the banana disappeared slowly into his mouth. I sat on his lap, removed the banana, and started undressing him.

"We have to go to class," he said, without offering any resistance.

"Later. I want to see more of the demonstration."

Afterward, I wondered why I had become so excited by Marcelo's banana trick. It certainly had nothing to do with performing fellatio myself. That was for his enjoyment, not mine. Rather, it was the idea of *him* doing it that was so provocative. It lent him an air of sexual ambiguity, increasing his already considerable attractiveness.

A week later, in bed, I asked, "Have you ever had sex with a guy?" He shook his head languorously, not seeming the least disturbed by the question. The answer disappointed but did not surprise me. "Have you ever been attracted to one?"

"Never. I have always loved women. Women's bodies are works of art." He rubbed his thumb gently against my clitoris. "But men's bodies?" He made a face. "They are like sour milk. If I were a beautiful woman like you . . ." He slipped a finger inside me, keeping his thumb where it was. "I would spend all my time making love to other beautiful women."

"Do you wish I were a lesbian?"

"Ah, but then you would not be here with me. And that would make me very sad." He pressed his eyes shut, as if to heighten his sense of touch. "You are so soft inside."

"Don't stop."

"Janna, are you telling me you like women?"

I smiled. "No. In fact, if I were a beautiful man like you, I would spend all my time making love to other beautiful men."

He laughed. "Then we are a perfect match."

I still made it to my grandparents' house every Sunday for dinner. Usually I went early to spend time with them alone, and to help with the cooking. When my dido was younger, he had taken pride in preparing the weekly meal. Now that he was approaching eighty, the brunt of the work fell on Baba, who was ten years his junior. One Sunday, after having spent the weekend with Marcelo, I was helping to make kashtan patties. Baba shaped the ground, seasoned meat into small balls around a dab of butter, then handed them to me to dip into egg batter and roll in bread crumbs. I felt the touch of her hand on my cheek, brushing away a piece of hair. "When I was little, they have a saying. A young girl is a rosebud. It is lovely, but closed." Baba drew her fingers together. "But when she falls in love, her petals open," she opened her hand, "and you see her true beauty." She waited a moment, then added mischievously, "Your petals are starting to show."

I could feel myself blushing. "*Nee,* Baba. I'm too busy at school for that."

"A pretty girl like you? It is not possible you don't have boyfriend. Maybe you do not tell me because he is not Ukrainian boy." I looked away, ashamed, even though I knew there was no reason to be. "Don't worry. I don't tell your parents. I prefer you like a Ukrainian boy, but . . ." she shrugged, "you like who you like. So, this boy, does he go to school with you?"

"*Tak.*"

"Then he is smart. That is good. What does he study?"

"Political science." Baba looked puzzled. "Government. Politics."

"Good, then maybe he becomes president of United States!" I said nothing, knowing that was an impossibility. "What about his family?"

"I haven't met them yet. They live far away."

"How far away?"

I took a deep breath. "Argentina."

"Oh, my goodness! Why not China?" She laughed. "I'll tell you a story. I never told this while my sister Kateryna was alive, but she is gone now, and her husband also, so there is no harm. Kateryna and I, we cross the ocean on a boat to come here to get married, I to your dido, and Kateryna to Uncle Vasyl. This is after First World War. The communists take over Russia, and everyone is worried what will happen. My parents, they arrange marriage for us. They know another family with two sons, your Dido and Uncle Vasyl. They left Ukraine before the war and are already American citizens, with good jobs. They are looking for wives. We never meet them, but we have their pictures and they write us letters. Kateryna and I travel with our father from Kiev to Odessa on Black Sea, to take a boat. When we say good-bye, Kateryna and I don't know we never see our parents again."

"Why didn't they come with you?"

"It is very hard to get into United States. Too many people want to come, and government sets a limit. But, if you marry American citizen, you don't have to worry. That is how Kateryna and I get in. Later, we try to bring our parents, but once Stalin comes, it is the end. He called it 'collectivization,' but truly it was murder. First he takes everyone's land. If you resist, they kill you or send you to Siberia. Then Stalin says Ukraine must make big increase in amount of grain they give to Soviet Union. And until grain quota is filled, no one in Ukraine is allowed food, not even the people working on the land. Communist officials come to your house anytime, day or night, and if they find one scrap of bread they say you are stealing government property and you get ten years hard labor. You cannot even imagine what people were eating—rotting garbage, diseased animals, cats and dogs, mice, bark from tree, grass, bugs. Millions of people die from starvation. Our whole family gone, parents, aunts, uncles, cousins. And before they die, how they suffer. You know what they look like, those people in German concentration camps?" I nodded cautiously. "That is what all of Ukraine looked like. People went crazy from hunger. Some murder for food. Others kill themselves, especially women, when their children die. And there is no one to bury the bodies because everyone is so weak they can barely move. And what did Russia do with all this grain they take from Ukraine? Sold to other countries, to make money. Sometimes they even let the grain rot! Can you imagine?"

"But why?"

"The Russian communists, they wanted to destroy Ukraine. We were different from them, and people hate what is different. They shut down our churches, our culture groups, our newspapers. They killed Ukrainian priests, intellectuals, and government leaders. They even went around with their guns shooting nightingales, because they are national symbol of Ukraine." Baba sighed. "Not that it was so good before the communists. When I was a little girl, and Tsar was still in power, there was a law you couldn't speak Ukrainian in school or in a public place. You had to speak Russian. How can you tell people they can't even speak their own language?"

I was glad my grandmother told me these things, because I needed to know. Still, it made me feel spoiled and guilty to think about how easy my life had been. "Baba, why are people so bad?"

"Only God knows the answer to that." Baba returned to methodically rolling meatballs. "Anyway, this is not the story I want to tell you. I want to tell you about how we come to America." Her tone lightened. "First, me and Kateryna, we have to take boat to Marseilles, France. There we change and take another boat to New York. We have never been to another country, so this is very exciting. On the second boat, me and Kateryna meet an American family—father, mother, and son. They are very wealthy. They travel first class. The boy, he likes Kateryna. And Kateryna, she likes the boy. They cannot speak one word in the same language, but never mind. They communicate. They make hand gestures, they draw pictures." Baba laughed. "Every night after dinner, Kateryna and the boy go walking on deck. I go as chaperon, because otherwise it looks bad. But I am really more like lookout. If I see anyone coming, I start singing the national anthem, so Kateryna knows. Every night they kiss and kiss. I stand away from them, but still, I know what is happening." It was hard for me to imagine my great-aunt Kateryna young and in love. From as far back as I could remember, Kateryna was a kind, elderly woman, so immensely fat she rarely left her seat in the kitchen.

Baba continued. "Kateryna meets the boy every night, for entire trip. Then, the last night, I see the boy point to his heart, then to Kateryna. Kateryna does the same. I think, now we are in trouble. That night she is crying because she knows next day she has to say good-bye. I feel bad for her, but there is no choice. She makes me swear I never tell anybody, especially our husbands, because if Vasyl finds out, he will be very angry. But he never does because I know how to keep secret." She made a gesture in front of her lips as if turning a key. "We get off the boat and look for our husbands. There are so many people, we don't know where to look. We have Ukrainian newspaper with us. We start waving it around. Finally they see us. I meet your dido, and I am very happy. He is young, good-looking, nice. But Kateryna, she got tricked. Her husband is much older than the picture they gave her, and he smokes cigar." She grimaced. "I think then she wishes she run off with the American boy." My grandmother sighed. "Kateryna and your Uncle Vasyl were married fifty years when he died. But sometimes, when Kateryna and I are alone, she says, 'You remember the boy on the boat? His face, so handsome! His hands, so clean. His hair, like gold. And his eyes, I will never forget those eyes.' When she says this, she smiles, but also she is sad. And then she asks, 'Do you think he remembers me?' I always tell her yes, because I think if I say no, it will break her heart. Anyway, I believe it. Something like this, you never forget."

The doorbell rang. I looked out the window. "Everyone's here."

My grandmother touched my arm. "I tell you this story so you understand. If you want to marry a boy from Argentina, marry a boy from Argentina. Don't end up like your Aunt Kateryna."

"Ya tebe kokhayoo." I love you, I exclaimed, losing myself in the soft, comforting contours of her body. The doorbell rang again. Slowly I withdrew, then went down the stairs to let in the rest of the family.

That evening, I went straight to Marcelo's from my grandparents' house. At his request, we watched *The Garden of the Finzi-Continis,* even though he said he had seen it many times. When the credits began to roll, Marcelo abruptly snapped off the TV. He had been quiet all evening. First I thought it was because of the somber subject matter of the film, but now I sensed there was another cause.

"Janna, I must ask you something." He was clearly agitated. "Every week you visit your family for dinner, and you have never invited me. Why is this?"

It had never occurred to me that he would want to come. "My parents . . ." I looked down, embarrassed. "They're difficult."

"Is it because I am not American?"

"American, African, Japanese, or Finnish. It's all the same if you're not Ukrainian."

"Why do you not stand up for me, and for yourself?"

"You don't understand. It's not that easy."

"I did not say it was easy, but if I meant enough to you, you would do it."

I thought hard about what I was going to say. I wanted to get it right. "I've always told myself I would save this battle with my parents until I met the guy I would . . ." I was going to say "marry" but did not want to scare him off. "Until I met a guy I thought would be in my life for a long time. You're graduating in the spring, and you haven't told me what you're going to do after that. If there's some possibility of a future together, I'll do whatever's necessary with my family. But if there's not, I don't see the point."

"That is fair." He sat down, seemingly lost in thought. "I have not lived in Buenos Aires for many years. When I visit, I am very, what is the word?" He looked to me for the answer.

"Homesick?"

"Yes, homesick." He leaned forward on the couch, placing his bony elbows on his knees. Although I was sitting next to him, I felt very far away. "I want to give something back to my country, and I cannot do that from here. Do you understand?"

"Yes. But where does that leave us?"

A small carved clock ticked softly from the bookcase. "I do not know. That depends on you."

"I have another year here."

"Yes," he said pensively.

"And even if I didn't . . ." I stopped. Was he asking me to move to Argentina with him? Was that something I would consider? "I don't even know how you feel about me."

He looked up, startled. "How could you not know how I feel? I love you," he declared earnestly.

"I love you too." I meant it, but somehow it sounded like an afterthought. It wasn't at all the way I had imagined the moment. "What happens now?"

"We wait and see."

It was not the answer I wanted to hear, but it was an honest one. It was only November. A lot could happen before Marcelo graduated in May. As it turned out, I didn't have to wait long. One afternoon shortly after our discussion, I went to meet him at a neighborhood café. When I arrived, he was sitting with a guy I didn't recognize. They both stood to greet me. "Janna," Marcelo said, "please meet my friend Christopher." After shaking my hand and exchanging a few pleasantries, Christopher politely excused himself.

"How do you know him?" I asked.

"We have had a few classes together."

"He's very cute."

"Should I be worried?" Marcelo gave me an untroubled grin.

"Oh, no. Not cute for me, cute for you."

His smile faded. "I do not understand."

"What I mean is, if you liked men, he would be a good match for you."

"But I do not like men. I have already told you this. And he is a friend. It is not right for you to say these things."

"Sorry," I replied, but he did not look convinced.

It should have ended there, but it did not. Two weeks later, we were walking up the stairs to Marcelo's apartment. A man passed on his way down. He and Marcelo locked eyes briefly and exchanged greetings. It was clear from the way the man had looked at Marcelo that he found him attractive. When we got inside, I said, "I think you have an admirer."

Marcelo dropped his keys on the table with a loud clunk. "Yes, I know." He sounded mildly irritated. "He lives in the building."

I knew I shouldn't say anything else, but I couldn't help it. "You know, if you decided to do it, it wouldn't bother me."

"Quite the opposite, I gather," he replied sharply. He had never raised his voice to me before. "Why do you keep saying these things to me?"

"I'm sorry."

"I do not want to hear that you are sorry. I want to know why."

I had no idea what to say. The whole thing was a stupid fantasy I should have kept to myself. I didn't really want Marcelo to be with men. It was merely the idea that he could be which I found exciting, and strangely comforting. I knew this wouldn't make any sense to him. It barely made sense to me. So I simply answered, "I don't know."

We stood by the door, our coats still on, looking at each other. I tried an expression of appropriate contrition, but when I could no longer take the weight of his eyes, I dropped my gaze to the floor. "What hurts me, Janna, is that you would want me to be with someone other than you, man or woman, it does not matter."

"It's not that."

"I do not think I have misunderstood. One time, maybe, but it is too many times now."

"I promise I won't do it anymore." I unzipped his jacket and ran my fingers down his chest. He looked away but did not stop me. Noticing the beginnings of an erection, I coyly stroked the front of his pants. After a few moments, he lifted my hand.

"It is not right for you to do this," he said in a choked voice. "I am angry at you."

"But if you are angry at me, how could you . . . ?" I glanced down at his crotch.

"That is not within my control. Please, Janna, you should go."

"OK," I replied meekly. "Can I see you this weekend?"

"I do not know." He said this sadly, as though wishing things were different. As I walked out the door, he called, "Wait." Briefly, I regained hope he would ask me to stay. "It is not safe for you to walk home alone. I will take you."

"That's not necessary." But Marcelo insisted, a gentleman to the end. We walked back to my dorm in silence. When we arrived, he did not go in with me, and he didn't kiss me good night. I stayed by the phone all weekend, but he did not call. The following week, I waited for him in the back row of the class we shared. It was the last session before the final exam, maybe my last chance to speak to him. Marcelo came in late. I gestured to the seat I had saved next to me, but he didn't take it. He asked me to wait for him after class, then moved away.

We left the building together, wandering directionlessly. Eventually he spoke. "I think we should stop seeing each other. I like you very much, but—"

"You said you loved me."

"I do." He paused. "I did." I felt my body sinking in on itself, like a rubber ball punctured by a metal cleat. "You do not know what you want, Janna."

"Yes, I do. I want you."

"No. You want to make me into something I am not, and that is not acceptable." He looked into the distance. "I wish it did not have to be this way." His sincerity made what he was saying all the more difficult. "I hope we can remain friends."

I nodded, knowing that was impossible. "Sure," I said in a small voice. "Sure."

≈≈≈

Until exams were over, I held out hope Marcelo might call, but he didn't. The next semester I saw him only once, from afar. I wanted to call him but didn't have the courage. I wrote him a dozen letters and tore up every one. He had made his feelings clear. Even if I could have won him back, in a few months he would graduate and return to Argentina. There seemed no point in risking almost certain humiliation for the chance of a brief reconciliation, after which I would probably never see him again.

I returned to my life with the triad. They were still entertaining, but I had less patience for their vulgarity after being around someone as refined and gracious as Marcelo. There had been one surprising and encouraging turn of events. Arthur had snagged a boyfriend. Craig seemed a nice enough guy, if a trifle shallow. Perhaps Arthur wasn't in love, but he did seem to be "in like." I found that rather touching in someone as disdainful of emotional involvement as he was.

One Saturday evening in early spring, the guys invited me to a party in a huge, tony apartment shared by two male students rumored to be lovers. When we arrived, the party was in full swing, crammed with the chic set from the university. Ian immediately disappeared, as was his fashion. I danced with Denton while Arthur and Craig hung out at the bar. After a half dozen songs, Denton went to get us drinks. As I was wiping my sweaty forehead with a napkin, a stunning blond approached. He introduced himself as Tom. We spoke for a few minutes until Denton returned. He and Tom exchanged greetings, then Tom stepped back into the crowd.

"You know that guy?" I asked, intrigued.

"Everybody knows Tom." He handed me a vodka tonic.

"What's his story?" I sipped the drink too quickly, desperate to cool down.

"He has a crazy girlfriend, but I don't see her here." He gave the room a once-over. "Anyway, she doesn't seem to care what he does, or who he does. Which is good, since he does them all—guys, girls, and in between. And let me tell you, they line up for it. In addition to being gorgeous, he's a really nice guy, and, I understand, quite accommodating." He took a swig of his drink while bopping to the music.

I eyed him suspiciously. "What's your source of information?"

"Secondhand, I'm afraid. I've only had the pleasure of his social company. Perhaps someday I'll have the honor of knowing him more intimately." He stretched out the last word in a comic exaggeration of his Southern drawl.

Later that evening, Tom crossed my path again. We danced to a few songs, the last one being a slow number. It felt good to be in a man's arms again. Four months had passed since my breakup with Marcelo, and this guy was attractive, sexy, and interested. Maybe a bisexual guy was the answer, someone who would desire me while still having that intriguing twist.

We ended up in the darkened bedroom of one of the hosts. At first we were only making out, but he was progressing quickly. Soon he was touching me in ways I had not let Marcelo do until after weeks of dating. I wanted him to slow down, but it was clear he had no intention of doing so. I wasn't sure what I had expected with a bisexual guy, but this wasn't it. If Tom was different from the straight men I had dated, it was only that he was more aggressive. That was the last thing I wanted, especially in a stranger. Part of me just wanted to give in and let it happen, but when I felt him edging down my pants, I asked him to stop. He did.

"What's the matter, hon?"

"I don't feel comfortable doing this." I looked nervously toward the door. "Someone could walk in."

"Door's locked," he said, running his tongue down the length of my neck.

I zipped up my pants. "I'm sorry."

"You want to go somewhere else?" he asked good-naturedly.

"No. This doesn't feel right to me."

"OK." He sounded surprised, but not upset. "Catch you later, then." He kissed me on the forehead and promptly left. I turned on the lights and fixed my disheveled clothing and hair. After making sure no one was in the hall, I slipped out of the room. I found Denton chattering with a mindless Eurotrash poseur we had nicknamed Ursula, because of her vague resemblance to Ursula Andress. It was not difficult to pull him away.

"You have to get me out of here. I'll explain later."

Denton led me out of the building and into a cab. "So what's all the cloak and dagger?"

"Ugh! I can't believe what I did." Glancing at the back of the cabbie's head, I lowered my voice. "I almost had sex with him."

"Tom?" he asked in awe. I nodded. "But why didn't you?"

"Denton, I barely know him! I shouldn't have let it go as far as it did."

"So," Denton asked inquisitively, "where did he go after you got him all hot and bothered?"

I glared at him. "Planning to pick up where I left off?" Denton was silent. "I can't believe you. Should I ask the cabbie to turn around?"

"No," Denton said with resignation. "It's too late anyway. He's bound to have found someone else by now."

The next day, I joined the guys for Sunday brunch. To my relief, they had finally abandoned the sleazy diner with the overendowed busboy for a popular student hangout. When I came in, I spotted Denton and Arthur in a booth. I slipped in next to Denton and grabbed a piece of his toast. "Where's Ian?" I asked idly.

Denton shrugged. "He said he'd join us, but you know how he is with punctuality."

"Not surprising, since he doesn't wear a watch." I crunched down on the toast.

"That's so he can ask cute guys in the street for the time."

I rolled my eyes. "Is Craig coming?" The waitress brought my coffee and refilled Denton's and Arthur's cups.

"No," Arthur replied. "And there's quite an amusing story behind it, actually."

"Do tell," Denton encouraged.

"We were getting ready to leave the party last night . . ." I had been trying hard to forget the party. At its mention, my feelings of regret returned, and I barely paid attention to what Arthur was saying. "I'm standing there waiting for Craig to come back with our coats. Who comes up to me but that hot blond, you know, the one with the crazy girlfriend, Tom something. He grabs my ass and asks if we can go someplace." I snapped out of my stupor to see Denton tightly shaking his head at Arthur. "What's the problem?" Arthur asked.

"It's OK," I said. "I want to hear this."

Arthur continued drolly. "I say to him, 'I would love to, but I'm here with somebody.' Tom asks me to point him out, which I do. Tom says, 'He's cute enough. I'll do both of you.' I say, 'That's fine with me, but I don't think he'll go for it.' Tom says, 'Don't worry.' He walks over to Craig and starts talking to him, up close in his ear. I can imagine what he's saying, because Craig looks like he's ready to drop his pants right there." Arthur laughed, a harsh, dry sound. "Actually, I was kind of surprised he agreed to it." He kept his eyes on his cigarette as he ground it slowly into the ashtray, then lit another. "We go back to Craig's place. Craig's roommate passes the three of us in the hall. He exchanges a look with Tom, which I think nothing of at the time. We go into Craig's room. Tom wants to do Craig first. Fine."

"Wait a minute," I interrupted. "You watched this guy screw your boyfriend?" Although I generally found the idea of men together exciting, the scene being related was too sleazy to evoke anything but my revulsion.

"Sure, why not?" Arthur replied, picking a piece of tobacco off his tongue. "Well, that is, I would have watched them. But I wanted a cigarette, and you know how Craig is about smoking, so I hung out in the kitchen until they were done." When Arthur spoke again, his voice was artificially loud and boastful. "Now, as you know, I don't really go in for being fucked. But this guy was so hot, there was no way I was going to turn him down." As Arthur had clearly intended, people from neighboring booths were staring. I slumped in my seat, hoping no one would see me. "Craig stayed, which was, uhm, awkward." This was said in a quieter tone, with considerably less bravado. "It's kind of weird having your boyfriend watch you get screwed when you're the one who's supposed to be doing the screwing. But I guess he was just there waiting for us to finish, because when we did, Craig asks Tom for another round. But Tom says he has to go. He gets dressed, goes to the can, takes a piss. After that we don't hear anything, so we figure he's gone home to screw the crazy girlfriend. Then I say to Craig, how about if *I* fuck you? But he says he's too tired." Arthur crushed another cigarette, even though it was only half done, and lit a fresh one. "Of course, he would've flopped on his stomach in a second if Tom had walked back in the room, but I suppose that's understandable." The table was painfully quiet. Denton chewed uneasily at the side of his mouth. I studied the gold flecks in the Formica tabletop. This was far worse than I could have imagined. "At that point, I decide to go." His tone picked up its former joviality. "As I'm walking down the hall, I see Tom disappear into the roommate's room." He slapped his hands on the counter. "Can you believe it? The guy comes in and fucks the whole house! Pretty amazing, huh?"

"Pretty disgusting," I mumbled under my breath.

"Why?" Arthur asked. "He's just giving people what they want. Nobody's complaining, I can tell you that."

"I'm sure that's true," I replied softly.

"Anyway," Arthur continued, "there's no way I'm going to miss the opportunity to tell Craig about this, especially since he was pissed the guy didn't do him a second time. I go back to Craig and say, 'Guess who's fucking your roommate?' Craig jumps up, runs over to his roommate's door, and starts pounding on it. The roommate comes out and they're cursing each other. Tom must've figured the party's over, because he zips up and heads for the door. You should have seen those two queens clawing at each other to get to him. Problem was, they couldn't follow him out in the hall because they're both stark naked. Once Tom's gone, these two really start going at it. Craig's yelling, 'How dare you steal my trick.' The roommate's yelling, 'You already had him. Why'd you have to ruin it for me?' Then Craig starts in with, 'And you still owe me last month's rent.' By now the neighbors are banging on the ceiling, so I booked out of there." Then Arthur added, almost to himself, "The way they were carrying on, you'd think I had already left, anyway." Arthur took a long drag from his cigarette, then expelled a thick stream of smoke. "Pretty amusing story, huh?" Denton and I said nothing. "What is the matter with you two? Janna we know has a stick up her ass—"

"Excuse me?" I shot back.

He ignored me. "But Denton, I've never seen such a constipated look on your face."

"Why doesn't everyone calm down," Denton suggested, seeing the anger percolating in my face. "There's something you don't know, Arthur. Before Tom came on to you last night, he was with Janna."

For a moment, Arthur looked stunned. Then he laughed uproariously. Again, people swerved their heads to look at us. "That's the crown jewel of the story. I couldn't have asked for anything better. But I'm surprised, Janna. Isn't he rather out of your league?"

It took a moment for the insult to sink in. When it did, I stood up and leaned over the table into Arthur's face. The words came quick, from somewhere outside of myself. "I wouldn't want to be in any league you're in, Arthur."

Arthur impassively flicked his ashes into the dented metal tray. "Don't kid yourself, baby, you already are."

On my way out the door, I ran into Ian. "Don't go yet," he said, "You'll miss a great story."

"Sorry," I replied, moving past him. "I've had my fill for the day."

I walked for a long time, contemplating my role in the events of the previous evening. They troubled me, as did Arthur's final comment. How could he say I was like him? I wanted things romantic and beautiful, not sordid and ugly. Was it my fault if things turned out ugly in the end? I knew I needed to make some changes in my life. What happened with Tom could not be repeated. And I had to get some distance from the guys, at least for awhile.

Getting distance from Arthur was easy. According to Denton, Arthur had no intention of ever speaking to me again, and true to his word, he never did. At first I was glad, but eventually I missed his acerbic humor and intelligent advice. I wrote him a short note of apology, even though I thought I deserved one from him. He never responded.

▲▲▼

Senior year was bleak. During the first semester I embarked on a disastrous affair with a PhD candidate in physics. When Frank approached me in yoga class, I was instantly put off. He had small eyes of an indeterminate color, an elongated nose, pale, thin lips, and hair that was badly in need of a cut. Although he was tall and thin like Marcelo, one would never think to compare the two. Marcelo had perfect posture, carrying his lean frame with grace and nobility. Frank slumped and dragged his scrawny body like an old, battered suitcase you couldn't wait to throw in a ditch. Reluctantly, I accepted his invitation for coffee, not wanting to reject him solely because of his looks. We spoke for an hour, or rather he did, explaining his theories on particle physics, doodling demonstrative sketches on a napkin. Although I hadn't the vaguest idea what he was talking about, I found him fascinating. Soon we were meeting regularly for lunch, then dinner. He seduced me with his intellect, and by the time he kissed me, those aspects of his physical appearance which I had initially found repugnant were almost attractive.

Frank's brilliance was intimidating. Secretly I wished I could be like him and felt inferior because I knew I never could be. I was so in awe of him that I overlooked his shortfalls, like how he always dominated the conversation and divided our restaurant bills to the penny. That my sexual needs were going unmet barely seemed worthy of notice, but his lack of affection was troubling. Desperate for his approval, I tried to mold myself into the kind of woman I thought he wanted. He had implied I talked too much, so I tried to be more reticent. He didn't like makeup, so I stopped wearing it. I cut back on time with my friends and my family, so I would be more available for him. I never even introduced Denton or Ian to Frank, afraid he would find them ridiculous and that the boys would lose respect for me for dating someone so ugly. Then, after only two months, Frank dumped me over bad Chinese, saying I was too "clingy." My devastation was unmatched by anything I had experienced. Although Marcelo and I had dated longer, and I was much happier with him, when we split, I was still me. By the time Frank left, I was nothing.

For the next few weeks I made an idiot of myself, telephoning him, sending impassioned letters, waiting for him outside of his building. At first he was merely brusque, then hostile. I gave up after seeing him exit his apartment one morning with another woman. She had a pockmarked face, stringy hair, and the kind of glasses your mom would pick out for you at thirteen. I rushed home to stare at myself in the mirror, wondering how awful my personality must be that he would prefer that woman to me. Humiliated, I retreated to my dorm room, venturing out as little as possible.

One evening, while I was checking out a book in the university library, I ran into Denton. "Girl, where have you been?" His voice was loud enough for the desk attendant to give him a reprimand. "You look terrible," he said, a little more softly. Then he gasped dramatically and lifted my face to the light. "Has Chanel gone bankrupt?"

For the first time in a long time, I could feel myself smile. "No. I'm just recuperating from a disastrous love affair."

"Good! Me too. Let's do go somewhere and cry in our beer."

We went to a local student bar. Sitting at a sticky table carved with graffiti, we exchanged our tales of woe. I told Denton about Frank, and Denton recounted his infatuation with an ostensibly straight student who, with some cajoling, let Denton give him a blow job, then ignored him. After we had excessively analyzed our doomed affairs, Denton said, "Darling, it is time to move on. I propose that tomorrow night we get dolled up and go out on the town."

I peeled the label off my third beer. "I'm not up for anything like that."

"You know this boy doesn't take no for an answer. I'll be at your room tomorrow evening, eleven sharp. And if you look like this when I come, I'll make you up myself. So unless you want the crazed transvestite look, you'd better reacquaint yourself with those makeup brushes."

When we parted I gave him a hug and couldn't let go.

"OK, dear. Let's not get all weepy. It's terrible for the complexion."

It felt good getting fixed up, and having a reason to do so. I hadn't gone dancing since meeting Frank, whose idea of a night out was eating at a burger joint. I had mixed feelings about going somewhere gay. My homoerotic fantasies had been in deep freeze since dating Frank. It was impossible to contemplate him with a man, and I was too obsessed with him to think about anyone else. Reassociating myself with that part of my emotional life meant not thinking about him for awhile, and I wasn't sure I was ready to do that. When Denton arrived, I told him I'd like to go to a straight club. He happily obliged, but when our cab pulled up to the curb and I saw the dull, suburban crowd, I changed my mind. "You know what, we look too good for this place. Let's go somewhere fun." We ended up at our favorite haunt. There, among the beautiful boys, I danced to the tribal music and felt myself slowly coming back to life.

◢◣◥

When graduation came, I said a tearful good-bye to Denton and Ian, who were moving to New York and California, respectively. I gave Denton the dog collar Arthur had loaned me so long ago and asked him to return it and give Arthur my best. Although I was sad to see them go, I was happy to be finished with college and ready to move on with life. It did not take long for disappointment to set in. College had been a hothouse experience—intense, dramatic, social. Life in the working world was quite different. I took a job as an analyst for an investment bank. The work was dull and the hours numbing. I was at the office from 9 a.m. to 10 p.m., six days a week, took a cab home to my tiny apartment, watched TV for a half hour, went to bed, then got up the next morning and did the same thing.

Within a few years, I had grown to detest my colleagues' competitiveness and a worldview that was limited to what appeared on the financial pages. I opted for a career change and tried to make a go at what I liked best. With my grandpop's help, I landed a job as an assistant chef in a midsized restaurant. My goal was to open my own place, but in the meantime, I wanted all the experience I could get. While I continued to work long hours, at least I enjoyed what I was doing. Still, I wished I had more time and opportunity to meet men. I became romantically involved with one of the restaurant's regular customers, but he wasn't interested in anything serious. I lived with a poet/taxi driver for a few months, but kicked him out when he lost his job and sat around the apartment smoking dope all day. I was even desperate enough to let my parents fix me up with a Ukrainian guy, but that went nowhere.

Then Ian died. I hadn't seen him since graduation. I learned of his death from Denton, who was sick himself. I remembered back to college, when we had heard the first reports of a "gay cancer." Denton had laughed it off, saying these were guys who did excessive amounts of party drugs and got screwed by ten men a night. Ian had bought into the theory that the whole thing was a scare, fabricated to stop gay men from having sex, and refused "on principle" to change his sexual habits. Arthur was the only one who considered the disease a possible threat, but his solution was simply to stay away from bathhouses and sex clubs. As a woman, I didn't think the disease was a threat to me, and my friends seemed, at the time, indestructible. In retrospect, our attitudes were shockingly stupid. But at the time, the crisis that would later define the decade was barely more than an item of idle gossip.

After Ian's death, I made a point of calling Denton more often and visiting when possible. On one of my trips, he mentioned seeing Tom, emaciated and almost unrecognizable, in a service center for people with AIDS. A few months later, Tom was dead too. I realized I might have met the same fate if I had given in to him at that party years ago. Hearing of his death, I did something rare for me—I prayed. I gave thanks for having been spared and also said a prayer for Tom. The passage of time had allowed me to see him for what he was, a perfectly nice guy who, as Arthur had said, simply gave people what they wanted. After all, he had stopped immediately when I asked him to, which was more than I could say for some guys. I wondered what kind of man he would have become had he been given the chance. As for Arthur, no one had heard from him. I imagined him in Berlin or Munich, far away from all the turmoil. Yet I feared that he, and countless others I had known but lost contact with, was either dead or dying.

᭡᭡᭡

By 1988, after working three years as a chef, I had saved enough money to start my own café. Opening day was one of the happiest of my life. Almost all of my family were there. It was one of the last times I saw my grandfather, who died of a stroke a month later.

Even though he was close to ninety, no one seemed prepared for his death, least of all Baba. Over and over she asked, "After fifty-five years of marriage, how could it end this way?"

My family thought it would be better for Baba to live with somebody. Both my dad and his sister, Aunt Tamara, offered to let Baba move in with them. She refused, wanting to remain in her own house. Since I lived close by, I tried to stop by every day and even spent the night occasionally. Our family still came over to her house for Sunday dinner, but my mom and Tamara now did all the cooking. Baba was fading, and within six months, she was gone too. Although I knew it was what she wanted—she had told me so—her death left me heartbroken. Baba was the one person I could always confide in. She knew the dynamics of our family, the pressures of working life, and the joy and sorrow of romance. I wondered if I would ever find another person who understood me so well.

After Baba's funeral, my parents told me my grandparents had left me their house. I couldn't believe it, even when I saw the will. It was a very valuable piece of property. Somehow it seemed wrong that I should get it, despite my dad's explanation that I was the only one in the family without a home. "The only thing your dido and baba requested," my dad said, "was that you not sell the house. It is for you to live in with your husband and children." He gave me a serious look. "Please do not wait too long."

Moving into my grandparents' house was a strange experience. Although it was like a second home to me, it seemed almost foreign without them. For a long time, I couldn't bring myself to clean out their closets, and so I kept my own clothes in the guest room. It was only when my mom offered to help that I forced myself to commit to the task. While my mom packed my dido's clothes, I went through Baba's closet. I remembered her fashion adages, repeated dozens of times over the years. "Black is good for someplace fancy. It's chic and makes you look slim." "Before you buy, check the lining. That tells you the quality." "For work, it's better to wear skirt and blouse. That way, you can mix them up. A dress may be pretty, but it always looks the same." As I folded the stylish clothes and placed them neatly in boxes, I thought how much I would miss these bits of Old World wisdom.

Later, when I moved my own clothes into my grandmom's dresser, I noticed a pair of shoes peeking out underneath. They were Baba's favorite dress pumps, black suede with a gold metal border at the heel. I picked them up and was about to place them with the other items going to Goodwill. Then I saw the imprint of Baba's foot on the inside of the shoe, as if she had just taken them off. It made it seem as if she would be coming back at any moment. I tucked them back under the dresser, where they always had been, and I hoped always would be.

◂◂◂

Toward the end of the year, I came home to a phone message telling me of Denton's death. The funeral and burial were in his hometown of Savannah, but his friends were planning a memorial service in New York. I did not attend. Not knowing Denton's other friends, I was afraid being there would only make me feel more alone. I remembered our last time together. Frail from a recent hospital stay and losing his sight, he walked around his apartment like a sleepwalker. "You know the one thing I regret?" he asked with a tired smile. "Not having a boyfriend. Now isn't that silly?"

"But what about . . ." I mentioned the name of a guy he had dated a few years back.

He shook his head. "No, I mean the real thing, true love and all that. Didn't know I was a romantic, did you? Must be the Southern belle in me. Well, I guess it doesn't matter much now, anyway."

I had wanted to tell him that I loved him, but I was afraid it would sound maudlin. Anyway, I knew that's not what he had meant. Now I regretted my silence.

A chapter of my life had come to a close, and in the pages that followed I saw nothing but stark white. I spent my free nights alone, in front of the TV. I loved the opera but was unable to find anyone to accompany me. Finally I decided to buy a solo subscription. During the first performance, I noticed a man a few seats down who was also by himself. We started talking during intermissions. Mostly we discussed the singers, but occasionally we exchanged personal information. At the end of the third opera, Winston asked if I wanted to go for a bite to eat, and I agreed. I was not particularly attracted to him. He was ten years older than I, and looked even older than that. But at twenty-nine, I was afraid my options were becoming limited. Winston was intelligent, erudite, and kind, and he possessed the two most important qualities in a man: he was single and employed. He wasn't a stranger to commitment, either. His marriage had lasted a dozen years and ended when he discovered his wife's affair with a neighbor. After three years of being single, Winston was ready for a serious relationship. It was hardly an opportunity I could ignore.

He pursued me ardently, wearing his emotions on his sleeve. Over time, I grew to care for him. He made me feel peaceful. It wasn't exactly the kind of relationship I had hoped for, but I wanted a family. I remembered the advice of a waitress at a restaurant where I had worked. "Honey," she said, "if you have to choose between a man who's in love with you, and one you're in love with, pick the first. It's the better deal." I had always hoped to find mutual love, but I was starting to wonder if that was a realistic goal.

Then Philip and Alex came along, symbolizing life's infinite possibilities. By reminding me of who I was, they gave me the determination not to compromise. Yet it wasn't clear what they offered me, if they offered me anything at all.

Pebbles

Janna called an employee to ask him to open the café, then dragged herself to the shower. The water beating down on her face helped clear her head, but only for a moment. Her thoughts drifted back to the night before, when Philip and Alex were in her bed. She reproached herself for having let such a thing happen, while simultaneously trying to recall every caress she had witnessed. The excited throbbing in her lower body returned, but she fought the urge to give in to it. She felt as if she were standing at a precipice. Nothing was visible over the edge except darkness.

As she got ready for work, she tried to ignore the many reminders of them throughout the house, but it was impossible. The acrid smell of rosin permeated the second floor, Alex's allergy pills lay scattered on the dining-room table, a six-pack of their Mexican beer crowded the refrigerator, and a kitschy male figurine in a hula skirt secured a grocery list to the kitchen cabinet. She had to find somewhere to escape. She picked up the phone, unsure whether she was desperate enough to go through with what she was contemplating. Then she caught a whiff of Philip's aftershave on the receiver. The scent was cool and clean, like the spray of a garden hose on a summer day. It was what she smelled every morning when she kissed his cheek. It was what Alex smelled every night when he kissed his mouth, slowly at first, growing more passionate until—"Stop it, stop it, stop it!" she yelled, violently ejecting the image from her brain. Grabbing a damp cloth, she wiped down the receiver and angrily punched in the numbers.

"Winston?"

"Janna?" He sounded surprised but pleased.

"Look, I'm sorry about storming out the other night."

"You had a right to. I was out of line. I wanted to call you to apologize, but when you said it was over—"

"I shouldn't have said that."

He was quiet a moment. "Does that mean you'll see me again?"

"I'll do better than that. Pack a bag for the weekend. Warm-weather clothes. I'll pick you up at six."

On her way out, suitcase in hand, Janna scribbled a note to the boys: Going away with Winston for the weekend. She considered adding, "We'll talk when I get back," but thought better of it. Maybe by then it would all be forgotten.

Saturday began with a shower of kisses. She opened her eyes to Winston's face bent over hers.

"It's nearly ten. Ready for breakfast?"

Despite the Bahamian sun streaming into the room, Janna's eyes slipped shut again. "I can't wake up."

"I'm not surprised after last night, Tarzana."

She smiled. It had been good, really good, too good. She gave herself credit for repressing all thoughts of Philip and Alex during sex with Winston. Until that time, though, she had been reliving the events of the previous evening almost continuously. She was on a roller coaster of arousal all day. It was especially bad during the plane ride. Each time there was a lull in the conversation, she drifted off into an intoxicating universe of memory. Where her memory got fuzzy, her imagination stepped in, taking her further and further every time. Then Winston would say something and jar her back to reality. The cycle continued until they reached the hotel. Although it was late, and she was tired, she jumped on him as soon as they were alone, thrilled to have a sanctioned release for her sexual energy.

At the beach that afternoon she relaxed under an umbrella, eating warm chunks of fresh pineapple cut in front of her by a local fruit vendor. The baking heat instilled a delicious sense of languor, a welcome respite after so many months of bracing northern air.

Settling back in a lounge chair, she scanned the beach until she spotted Winston at the ocean's edge, cruelly exposed in his bathing trunks. She wondered why she was so critical of him. He had a lot of positive qualities, not the least of which was his skill in bed. But it was not enough for her to desire the sex, she wanted to desire him. Then again, when she dated men she found attractive, they almost always turned out to be lousy lovers, selfish, egotistical, and lazy. The one exception was Marcelo. Surely he couldn't be the only one.

Janna almost expected to see Philip and Alex among the tourists on the beach sauntering by in colorful bathing trunks. The picture she conjured of Alex made her laugh, his long skinny legs jutting out of a speedo. She spied a young man in surfer shorts emerging from the sea. Thinking how good those would look on Alex, Janna imagined him in the man's place, water streaming off his body, oversized trunks clinging wet to his hips and thighs. An inexplicable desire overtook her. She wished she could be Philip, if only for a moment, so she could strip those shorts off Alex, feel his ocean-chilled skin beneath her warm hands, and make love to him in a way physically impossible for her as a woman. The impulse frightened her in its intensity and bizarreness, the worst part being that it didn't feel bizarre at all. It was with relief that she greeted Winston when he returned to the umbrella.

When they came back on Sunday evening, Janna accompanied Winston to his home and did not leave. As the days passed, it became easier to minimize what had happened with Philip and Alex, but she knew that would change once she saw them. She couldn't avoid them forever, though. They showed up at the café midweek. Janna was at the counter, filling out a purchase order. She kept her eyes on the form.

"We're sorry to bother you," Philip said, "but you haven't been home all week. Is everything OK?"

"Everything's fine. I've been staying with Winston." Her pen remained poised over the form, moving in small, jittery circles.

"You're not avoiding the house because of us, are you?" Alex asked.

"No, of course not." To Janna's dismay, her hand holding the pen began to shake.

Philip reached over and covered her hand with his. "Don't you think we should talk about this?"

They walked a few blocks to Rittenhouse Square. It was the best-maintained park in Center City, surrounded by venerable hotels and posh apartment buildings. One end bordered Curtis, and if it were any other time of year, Janna would be worried about bumping into Winston. In this frigid weather, though, that was hardly a concern. They sat on a bench in the deserted square, Janna on one side of the boys. Alex had his hands jammed in his pockets and was hunching his shoulders against the cold. Philip looked only slightly less miserable. "When are you two going to learn to wear hats? And I suppose you've lost your gloves again, Alex?" He nodded. "Come on, Philip, your boy is freezing. Do something to warm him up."

"Give me your hands, baby." He rubbed Alex's chapped hands in his, then tried to get Alex to take his gloves. After some good-natured quarreling, they split the pair. Philip clasped Alex's ungloved hand in his, then put them both in his coat pocket. At that moment, Janna realized how absurd it was to think a trip to anywhere would change her feelings. She'd gladly give up a lifetime of days at the beach to remain here, in the icy cold, watching these two hold hands.

"Look, guys, I feel very uncomfortable about what happened last week."

"But nothing happened. You saw us fool around a little, you conked out, and we went back to our room. Perfectly harmless." As he spoke, Philip's breath formed small gossamer clouds that dissipated the moment they became visible.

"How'd I get in bed?"

"We carried you. You don't remember?"

"Not really."

"I promise, your virtue was not compromised." The excessive gravity of his voice, coupled with the upturned corners of his mouth, showed he was mocking her, although not without affection.

She leaned back against the hard wooden bench, shaking her head pensively. The skin on her face felt tight and dry. "My virtue. Now there's something I haven't seen for a long time."

"You're making way too much out of this." A hint of annoyance had crept into Philip's voice. "You like seeing us together. Big deal."

A raw gust of wind sliced through the park. Alex's quietness concerned her. "How do you feel about this?"

Alex raised an eyebrow. "It's a little weird, but . . ." He shrugged. "Whatever."

"Whatever?" she asked with dismay. "Whatever?" She waited for someone to say more, but no one did. So this was it? This was how they were going to leave it? After a few more minutes of unbearable cold, she stood. "I've got to get back." She took off her hat—her grandfather's Persian lamb—and placed it on Alex's head. "Give it back to me tonight. I'll be home."

It was a chilly morning, the kind that made it tempting to loll under the covers all day. Janna reached her arm out of bed to draw curlicues in the frost on the window. She was reminded of those mornings long ago when she'd awaken to the miracle of an overnight snowstorm and tune in to the radio for the announcement every child in the city was waiting to hear: "All Philadelphia public and parochial schools will be closed today due to the weather." After her mother packed her in a snowsuit, Janna would grab her tin sled and rush to a nearby lot where she'd race with the neighborhood kids down bumpy hills until her sister Larisa dragged her home for lunch. Even now, when she awoke to a big snow, there would be a flash of excitement before the reality of adult life, and shoveling the sidewalk, set in.

She lumbered out of bed and pulled on the clothes she had left in a pile on the floor the previous night. Not having the heart to evict the boys from her bed, she had spent the night here, in their room. Her inconclusive talk with them a few days earlier had left her unsure whether their little performance had been a one-time deal, or something more. She hadn't even known whether she wanted it to happen again. Now that it had, she found herself both elated and scared. She told herself she felt guilty, too, because of Winston, but she knew deep down she didn't.

The boys were still asleep when she entered her bedroom. Awash in sunlight and framed by her pale yellow sheets, they looked like angels ascending to heaven. She wondered if the comforts of her oversized bed were the incentive for their nighttime visits to her room. But perhaps she was being too cynical. If they had another motivation, though, did that make it better or worse? She touched Philip's naked shoulder. "Hey sleeping beauties, it's seven o'clock." They both groaned and, eyes still shut, rolled over on their sides. Philip threw an arm across Alex's chest. Seeing them like this stirred memories of the previous evening. Nevertheless, Janna successfully fought the temptations of the shower and got dressed and ready for work. When the boys left, though, she went back up to her room with resignation and locked the door. As she flung off her clothes, she had the sense she was crossing a bridge over which she would never be able to return. Images of the boys' lovemaking flooded her mind as her fingers released the frustration trapped in her body. Afterward, she felt as though every bone had been shattered and every muscle torn. She wondered, when this adventure ended, as surely it would, and soon, whether there would be anything left of her.

⌇⌇⌇

It lasted mere weeks, and happened only a handful of times, but each time was as brightly polished in Janna's memory as beach pebbles displayed in a seaside shop. She never knew when they would come to her, or what would take place when they did. The uncertainty was maddening. At night, she'd stand in her bathroom, wondering whether to wash off her makeup. Then she'd sit on her bed, waiting for their footsteps on the stairs, feeling like a rejected suitor if they chose their room over hers.

On the nights they did stumble into her room, three sheets to the wind and fighting over the TV clicker, she'd retreat to the same corner she had taken refuge in that first night, as much out of courtesy to them as a concession to her own modesty. She made one sole request, that they keep the covers to their waists. Philip teased her for being prudish. She tried to explain that she preferred some things left to the imagination. Although they seemed not to believe her, they abided by her wishes.

Repeated exposure helped soften her embarrassment, while leaving undiminished the hypnotic beauty of seeing the two men she loved love each other. There were certain acts, though, that she was not initially prepared to witness. The first time Philip tore open a condom wrapper, she quickly excused herself. The second time, she stayed, figuring she could leave if she became uncomfortable, but she never did. Between the darkness of the room and the covers on the bed, everything was softly obscured. What Janna could see was the graceful play of muscles in Philip's back, shoulders, and arms as he supported his body above Alex, who was prone beneath him, legs parted and wrapped back around Philip like embracing arms. After hearing so many revile this particular act, Janna was struck by how simple and natural it seemed. Every so often Alex twisted his face backward so Philip could kiss him, allowing Janna to glimpse briefly the force of a passion that seemed to renounce all constraints, even those of the human body. She recalled the impossible desire she had felt so profoundly for Alex that day at the beach. Although this seemed the most reasonable time for such an unreasonable desire, to her relief, she did not reexperience it. Those thoughts now struck her as an insult to Philip's legitimate desire for his lover, something Janna had no wish to encroach upon.

There was a sole impediment to her enjoyment. She hated that they allowed her to be there. It seemed a corruption of, or at least an intrusion upon, their intimacy. She wished there was some way she could be part of the experience, yet not change it by her presence. To be there, but not be there.

She didn't share these thoughts with them, nor did they discuss how they felt with her. This concerned her. For one thing, she sensed Alex was not as comfortable as Philip with their "arrangement." She knew she should raise the subject but was unable to muster enough courage. She also worried that they viewed her as an object of pity or, equally abhorrent, a voyeur. She shuddered at the image the word conjured of a dirty old man, or a miserable young one, who has no recourse to sexual pleasure other than peeping through his neighbor's venetian blinds. But her experience was so far removed from this. Her interest was not in watching men engage in sex acts. She had seen gay pornography in college, and it repelled her, as did most heterosexual pornography. What appealed to her, both romantically and erotically, was the expression of love, trust, and tenderness between two men, their desire for true intimacy, physical and spiritual, and their willingness to make themselves vulnerable enough to achieve it. She knew this type of relationship was as rare in gay couples as in straight and, therefore, was doubly grateful to have found a couple like Philip and Alex, in whose relationship these elements appeared to be not only present but flourishing.

Being around Philip and Alex helped Janna understand why she found gay male love so compelling. Although she could watch them have sex, she would never really know what they felt for each other. This allowed her the freedom to idealize their relationship and imagine a passion far beyond her experience. It was why she loved listening to them whisper in bed, so soft as to be inaudible. It was like opera. She spurned librettos and subtitles, preferring to know only the general outline of the story. For Janna, an opera was not sung in Italian, French, or German. It was sung in the universal, sublime language of music, which neither required nor was capable of translation.

Despite her romanticized view of Philip and Alex's relationship, she knew they were only human and, even worse, young and male. She heard them argue occasionally, and those arguments had become more frequent and heated since her return from the Caribbean. Although their disputes did not appear to have anything to do with her, she still worried she was the cause of growing discord between them.

Alex seemed especially tense. He had been working late for a week on some hideous piece of music, playing the same cacophonous phrases over and over, until Janna thought she would lose her mind. Philip didn't comment on the noise, but she noticed that increasingly he wore headphones around the house. One evening, Janna lifted the set from his ears and asked, "Is it supposed to sound like this?"

Philip laughed. "I dare you to ask him that."

"What's going on with him?"

"I don't know, but whatever it is, he'll get over it."

"I hope it's soon."

That night Janna awoke to what sounded like a deaf child banging on the piano. She waited five minutes and, when it did not stop, put on a robe and went downstairs. "Alex, honey, it's two o'clock. Can't this wait until the morning?" When he did not respond, she tried again. "Alex?"

His head snapped up. "Why are you interrupting me?"

Her face tightened. "You're playing too loud. It's keeping me awake."

"Since you're up anyway, come over here and play this for me."

Janna blinked her eyes in disbelief. "Now?"

"Of course now."

Although infuriated, she did as she was told. He shoved a stack of scribbled paper at her. She flipped through it. "I can't play this. It's an orchestra score. There are lines for cellos, oboes, horns—"

"You just pick out the melody."

"There's a melody?" she asked, incredulous.

"Just do it," he demanded. She tried her best, playing painfully slowly. "This isn't a funeral march. It's allegro. Here!" He stabbed the page with his finger.

"I see your tempo marking. I told you I can't do this. And you don't need me to. There's nothing I'm doing you can't do ten times better." She stood up and slammed down the keyboard lid. "And there's a new rule. No more music after midnight. If that's a problem, leave."

She pushed past Philip, who stood in the doorway half dressed and half asleep, asking, "What the hell is going on?"

The next morning Janna, who was not in the mood for confrontation, waited in her room for them to leave. Although the front door opened and closed a few times, she could tell someone was still in the house. Then she heard a strange scraping noise. A sheet of paper appeared under the crack of her door. The note was in Alex's scrawl: Please give me a chance to apologize.

Janna opened the door to Alex holding a sad bunch of flowers, which he timidly offered her. "I'm really sorry about last night. You should throw me out."

"I will, if you ever do anything like that again."

"I won't. I swear. I was just having such a hard time with that piece." She scrutinized him over the flowers, trying to deduce the real reason he had lashed out at her. "Anyway, Philip and I were planning on going out tomorrow. I've just about finished the symphony—"

"Thank God."

He smiled ruefully. "We wanted to invite you to come along, if you can still stand being around us."

"I don't want to interfere in your evening."

"You won't. I promise."

They went to a small club of the boys' choosing. The bar was at the front, and so crowded they had to force their way through. On the other side were banquettes, café tables, and a busy dance floor. There was a large screen showing music videos, clips from old movies, cartoons, commercials, and coverage of men's diving from the last Olympics. A persistent, throbbing beat filled the room, reflecting and amplifying the erotic energy that surrounded them. Janna hadn't been to a gay club since college, and although the music was different, the rush of excitement and nervous anticipation remained unchanged.

Janna allowed herself to be cajoled by Philip and Alex into dancing to a few songs. She was amused to see that Alex, a master of rhythm on the written page, had none of it on the dance floor. Yet his clumsiness had an endearing quality, and Philip, who was quite a good dancer, didn't seem to mind at all. They may not have been the most graceful couple on the floor, but they were certainly the sweetest.

Philip went to the bar, leaving Janna alone with Alex. They leaned against the wall and watched the video screen for awhile. "This place is nice. Do you guys come here a lot?"

He shook his head. "I'm not real keen on parading Philip around a place packed with humpy men."

Janna was surprised. "I can't imagine Philip looking at other guys."

"We all look. That's not what I'm worried about." Philip emerged from the crowd flanking the bar. "Watch how many guys check him out." A lot of guys did look at Philip, hardly a shock to Janna after the attention he received at the café. One attractive man engaged him in a brief conversation. "Long-lost friend?" Alex asked tartly when Philip returned.

"He seemed to think so." After handing them their beers, Philip put his arm around Alex and whispered something in his ear. Alex's sulky expression dissipated, and the two of them were soon laughing and dancing again.

They returned late. The silence of the house was a relief after the noise of the bar, which still drummed in Janna's ears. The boys raided the refrigerator while Janna warmed some sake on the stove, hoping it would take the bitter edge off the beer and help her sleep. She poured the liquid carefully into a china flask and placed it, together with a small cup, on a tray. On her way upstairs she passed Philip and Alex, who were sitting in the dining room, wolfing down roast-beef sandwiches. She said her good nights, not expecting to see them again that evening. As she prepared for bed, her thoughts turned to Winston. She had canceled plans with him that night to be with Philip and Alex, saying she had to baby-sit for her sister. She felt awful about lying. She felt awful about a lot of things. Maybe she wasn't technically cheating, but she felt emotionally unfaithful, and that was just as bad. Part of her wanted to tell Winston everything, to confess the double life she had been leading, but that would serve no purpose other than to hurt and confuse him, and he didn't deserve that. She knew she had to choose, but both alternatives were so terrifying, for such different reasons, that she couldn't bring herself to do it. What was certain was that the situation could not continue as it was.

There was a knock. Janna stuck her head out of the bathroom to find the boys standing in the bedroom doorway.

"Is it OK if we sleep here tonight?" It was the first time they had actually asked.

"Sure." Janna finished leisurely in the bathroom. As she was about to leave, she slipped a bathrobe over her T-shirt. Then, figuring she might as well enjoy this in style, exchanged the cotton and terry cloth for a silk nightgown and robe. She considered taking the sake with her, but drinking during this seemed a little too ancient libertine, even for her. She tossed back one more cupful of the warm liquid and stepped into the bedroom. The boys were under the covers and all over each other. She curled up in an armchair near the bed, deciding that for once she would watch without guilt, self-reproach, or timidity. The boys' frantic groping abated and their caresses became more prolonged. They were face to face, Alex on top of Philip. As Alex touched and kissed him, Janna saw Philip's normally assertive demeanor ease away, and his face take on an expression of blissful surrender. Janna had seen that expression, or a variation of it, on Alex, but it affected her differently. Alex's boyish face was made for expressions of surrender. Seeing that look on Philip's masculine face, and watching him yield so completely to his lover, awakened something previously untouched in Janna. But that something was just beyond her reach, like a dream only partly recalled, and awaited another occasion to be fully realized.

The position in which they ultimately made love, with Philip's heels resting on Alex's shoulders, struck Janna as incredibly awkward, if not downright ugly. She thought back to her college friend Arthur, whose favorite quip whenever an attractive man walked by was, "I'd love to see his legs in the air." She finally knew what he meant. Similarly, Arthur's focus on the attractiveness of men's feet, which Janna had never fathomed, now became understandable, given how close they were to the face during this particular act.

Because of their position, Philip and Alex were completely exposed. Janna chose not to follow the action of their bodies, which she found more mechanical than erotic. Instead, she allowed herself the more intimate experience of watching them watch each other's faces become transfigured by deepening shades of desire and pleasure. As the rhythm of their bodies accelerated, Alex leaned over to kiss Philip, almost folding him in two. A few moments later, Alex pulled back, his face tightening then relaxing into ecstasy. When they separated, Janna rose and moved toward the door, although with reluctance, as she felt profoundly close to them.

"Janna," she heard Philip say behind her. "Don't go. It's your bed, and it's big enough."

She hesitated, but the request seemed sincere and devoid of any sexual overtones. "Alex?"

In his postcoital state, Alex looked like he would have agreed to almost anything. "Sure, why not," he said, rubbing the back of his neck and yawning.

She slipped into the far corner of the bed and quickly fell asleep. Sometime later, she awoke to sound and movement indicating Philip and Alex were not done with each other. Alex was invisible beneath the covers, but from the position of his head and the clouded look in Philip's eyes, there was little doubt what they were doing. Janna got up to leave. Philip grabbed her hand, pulled her to him, and kissed her. It was neither a chaste kiss nor a passionate one. Innocently curious, perhaps. They kissed a second time, a little longer, but as they separated, Janna saw Alex exiting the bed. "Shit," Philip said as he got up to run after him.

Janna remained where she was, uncertain and guilt-ridden. She touched her lips tentatively. Of course, she had considered that this, and maybe more, might happen. She had even fantasized about it in a vague sort of way. But after having lost two friends to AIDS, she decided it simply wasn't worth the risk, assuming anyone wanted her to take it. Besides, it was disturbing enough that they let her watch. Any further participation would destroy the very intimacy that she wished to share. And it wasn't only her romanticized idea of gay love that would be a casualty, to which the raised voices in the next room attested.

"I knew it," Alex said, enraged. "I knew that's where this was going."

"It was only a kiss."

"No touching, no kissing. You promised."

"I know. I'm sorry. I got carried away."

"What did you have in mind, Philip, some kind of three-way? Should I have asked her to blow you while I fucked you? Is that what you wanted?" The ugliness in Alex's voice made Janna shudder.

"Please, Alex, stop this. She can hear you."

"Good," Alex shouted. "I want her to hear me." Janna covered her ears, but she could not block out his voice. "She's a fucking pervert," he roared, so loud Janna was afraid the neighbors would call the police. "And so are you, or you wouldn't let her do this."

"You said you were OK with it."

"If that's what you want to believe." There was the sound of drawers being yanked open and shut.

"What are you doing?"

"I can play the same game as you, Philip, only I guarantee I won't be playing it with a girl." He spat out the last word like it was a piece of filth.

What came next was a jumble of confused sounds: scuffling, a thud against the wall, a sharp grunt, someone racing down the steps, the front door slamming. Silence followed. Some time later, Janna looked up from her huddled position on the bed to see Philip. His face was ashen, his eyes unfocused, and his nakedness, which usually awed her, made him look painfully vulnerable.

She dried her eyes roughly with the backs of her hands. "What happened?"

He was quiet for a moment, and when he spoke, it was in a near whisper. "I was trying to stop him from leaving. He . . . he slammed me against the wall. Then, it was like an automatic reaction." A minute passed, but he did not continue.

"Philip?"

Slowly he raised his eyes to hers. "I hit him."

Astronauts

I was fourteen when we met. It was at a reception in New York following a violin competition in which I had taken first prize. I was wandering the hall, trying not to care that one of the preeminent managers of classical musicians in the country had just heard me play. While I was getting a soda at the bar, someone touched my shoulder. It was my dad, with *him*. He was about my father's age, forty-five or so, with a hint of silver in his dark hair and the remnants of an athletic build. He was impeccably dressed in a dark suit and silk tie and smelled like the woods after a spring rain.

When my father introduced us, *he* smiled strangely, as if he had just seen something unexpected. "I've been following your progress for some time, young man. I'm impressed."

His praise made me uneasy. I thanked him and tried to move away. My father stopped me. "Alex, where are your manners?"

"Let him go," he said with an affectionate chuckle. "But have him come by my office tomorrow."

The next day I arrived at his 57th Street office, violin in tow. I gawked as I entered the building lobby, pink marble and ten stories high, with a huge central fountain surrounded by tropical plants. His company's offices, which were on the fiftieth floor, were equally imposing. The walls were paneled in gleaming, dark wood. Fresh flowers were on every table. The furniture looked like it belonged in a museum. After giving my name at the desk, I teetered nervously on the edge of a chair in the reception area, waiting. Through the picture window, I could see all of New York City spread out before me. My mind drifted off into fantasies of record deals and sold-out concerts. Then I heard my name called.

He got right down to business, asking me to play a Bach partita and a Paganini caprice. It was standard repertory stuff, so I felt pretty confident. He sat behind his desk, facing the window. I couldn't see his expression while I played. When I finished, he nodded. "Technically proficient, but lacking in emotion." He spun his chair around to me. "Play something of your own." Without much thought, I chose the piece that had won me the New York Philharmonic's concerto competition. He stopped me after a few bars. "I've heard that. Give me something else, something more personal." I searched my memory, finally deciding on a moody rhapsody I had composed a few months earlier. Structurally simplistic, it was a risky choice, but I gave it a shot. When I was done, he looked at me the way my dad did when he was getting ready to yell. My heart pounded as I prepared for the onslaught. "That was excellent. You need to give that kind of depth to everything you play." He spun back toward the window, leaving me stunned. "I hope you'll let me represent you."

"I would be thrilled to have anyone in your company—"

He cut me off. "Me personally."

This was beyond anything I could have imagined. I didn't know what to say. "I guess you should talk to my parents."

"What do *you* want?"

No one had ever treated me like this before, like my feelings mattered. "I want you."

From the start, we met with unusual frequency. I came up from Philadelphia to New York every Saturday to attend Juilliard's program for precollege students. After my lessons, I'd stop by his office. Sometimes I'd play for him or show him a composition I was working on, but mostly we talked. He wasn't anything like my last manager. He didn't push me to perform too frequently and seemed genuinely concerned about my development. He also supported my artistic choices. When I requested classical guitar lessons from my parents, they refused, saying it would distract from my other studies. When I mentioned it to him, he immediately arranged lessons with a well-known teacher. We had a special relationship. He took me to the Hard Rock Cafe for burgers, Serendipity for frozen hot chocolate, and when I told him I was a basketball fan, we were sitting courtside at the next Knicks game.

It was nice having someone pay attention to me. I got so little from my parents. They didn't care about my success as much as they expected it. My father, a first violinist in the Philadelphia Orchestra, practiced and taught all day and worked most evenings. Other than the minimal time I was allowed for homework, he expected me to be in my room practicing from the moment I got home from school to the moment I went to bed. If I took a bathroom break, his voice would boom up the stairs, "Alex, I can't hear you." The flush of the toilet was my reply. My mother was a well-known musicologist. She commuted several days a week to teach at Juilliard. The rest of the time she was in her study, with a handmade "Do Not Disturb" sign hanging on the door. Our only interaction was the ninety-minute train ride we took to and from Juilliard every Saturday. She always carried a briefcase jammed with papers and was working before the train left the station. If we said more than three sentences to each other during the trip it was remarkable. Once we arrived at Juilliard, she disappeared into the sterile corridors, and I didn't see her until it was time to catch the evening train. We didn't speak about what I did in the afternoons once my lessons at Juilliard were over. I never told her I went to see him, worried she'd reprimand me with my father's favorite adage, "Any time spent doing something else could be spent practicing."

As time passed, my feelings for him became more intense and confusing. I was pretty naive about adult emotions. I lived in an insular world where the topics of conversation were how well you were mastering the Shostakovich, who placed where in the last competition, and whether you preferred Perlman's recording of the Dvořák Violin Concerto to Stern's. Professionally I was expected to act like an adult, but in every other way I was a child. Still, I knew what it was like to have a crush. There had been a few boys in my junior high I had liked. I'd stare at them across the room and imagine us rolling around naked together. But what I felt for him was different. I wanted him to hold me and take care of me. I wanted to be important to him. I wanted him to love me.

Two months had passed since our first meeting. He had arranged for me to play the Mendelssohn Violin Concerto at Carnegie Hall with the New York Youth Symphony. I was nervous but played well. Afterward there was a party. My parents bowed out early to return to our hotel, but they allowed me to stay. There was a lot of champagne, and I drank too much of it. Somehow I ended up with him alone in an apartment, too dazed to ask where we were, or why. When I saw the bed, all I could think about was how much I wanted to lie down. His hands on the back of my neck felt good, cool against my skin. He unbuttoned my shirt gently, like a father undressing a child. But then his tongue was in my mouth, and his hands were everywhere. I felt like I was on an amusement park ride that had gone out of control. Unable to breathe, I tried to pull my mouth away, but he only gripped me tighter. He yanked my pants down. I had an erection, which he brushed carelessly with his hand. I wanted to tell him to stop, but I had never been touched there before and it felt good. A moment later I was being pushed backward onto the bed. I heard the sound of his zipper and then blinding pain as his body ripped into mine. I screamed and kicked with wild panic, but he clamped his hand over my mouth and whispered, "Hold still."

When it was over, I curled around a pillow, too stunned to cry. He tried to comfort me, but I pulled away, unable to bear his touch. When he left the room, I sat up slowly, pain radiating throughout my body. It was then I saw the blood on the bedspread, a bright spot of crimson that seemed to grow as I watched it. I pulled on my clothes and darted past him, out of the apartment and down a corridor. Frantically, I looked for the elevator, but I couldn't find it. I took the fire exit, tripping down fourteen flights of stairs. On the street, I was disoriented and wandered for a few blocks before I saw a cab. During the ride to the hotel, I was overwhelmed by feelings of humiliation and betrayal. I rushed through the hotel lobby, the champagne burning my stomach like sugared turpentine. In the room, I fell to my knees in front of the toilet as bile exploded from my mouth. My parents didn't stir. Finding me the next morning on the bathroom floor, they said I'd gotten what I deserved for drinking so much. It never would have occurred to me to tell them what had happened.

I didn't go to see him the following week, or the next. Then one morning I noticed a dark sedan parked across the street from my house. I thought nothing of it until the same car showed up later at school. The next day, it was there again. I couldn't see through the smoke-colored windows, but I knew it was him. I was upset, not because I was frightened, but because I wanted to forget, and he wouldn't let me. By the third day I was angry. I was shooting hoops with some neighborhood kids when he pulled up. I waited until the game ended, then walked over to his car, stopping a few feet away. The door opened, and we stared at each other, him in an Italian suit and sunglasses, me in running shorts and tank top, basketball under my arm.

"What do you want?"

"To talk to you," he said gently, gesturing to the seat next to him.

I didn't move. "So talk."

"Not in the street."

"Leave me alone!" I shouted, backing away. I wanted to ask "Why?" but didn't have the nerve.

"Alex, please talk to me. I came all this way to see you." His voice was tender and desperate. He glanced pleadingly at the seat again. I hesitated, then got in, watching the playground recede through darkened windows as we pulled away.

We drove in silence for a while. When he spoke, it was stiff and formal. "Alex, you must forgive what I did. I drank too much that night and was not in my right mind. It will not happen again." He turned to face me. "You're very important to me. Do you know that?" I didn't respond. "Look in the backseat." I turned around to see a pile of gifts. Mostly it was stupid stuff, like sweaters and an ugly watch I later found out cost thousands of dollars. But he did give me a new fiddle case, a box set of Stravinsky's works, and floor seats to see Michael Jackson. I had never been to a rock concert before.

He kept his promise for a month. Then it happened again, in his office, on a deserted Saturday afternoon. One moment he was showing me how to play an electronic game he had bought me, the next he was pinning me to the couch. I'm not sure which was worse, the first time drunk or the second time sober. He was extremely affectionate afterward, holding and petting me, like I had imagined him doing before, murmuring "I'm sorry" over and over.

I stopped fighting him. It was useless and only made it hurt worse. I also stopped practicing and composing. I skipped school and faked my way through lessons. He was upset when he found out, which pleased me immensely. My parents grounded me but weren't around to enforce it. They cut off my allowance, which was a joke. Any money I needed I'd lift from his wallet, right in front of him. At first I felt guilty about it, then I figured I might as well take what I could from him, because he was sure as hell taking everything from me.

When I was in his office, photographs of his teenage daughters watched us from the wall. There was no picture of his wife, but his wedding band confirmed her existence. I felt sorry for her, but jealous of the daughters, imagining they got all his love without the brutality. One evening, after the usual, I passed the pictures on my way out of his office. Something about their expressions made me feel like they were laughing at me. I reached up and calmly knocked them off the wall. Startled, he looked down at the splintered glass but said nothing.

The next week, his driver picked me up from Juilliard to meet him for a late lunch. He did that sometimes—took me to ridiculously expensive restaurants where I played with my food and everyone treated me like his son. He was on the phone when I came in. "Yeah, I'm getting ready to talk to him." He hung up and turned to me. "That was Dorothy. She's livid."

"What's the big deal? I showed up."

"And she's supposed to be grateful for that? If you come to one more lesson unprepared, she's dropping you."

"Who cares?" I put my feet up on the chair. He pushed them down.

"You do, if you're interested in having a career as a violinist."

"Maybe I'm not."

He looked surprised. "You're going to study composition full-time?"

"I didn't say that."

He narrowed his eyes. "Don't tell me you're giving up the violin for the *guitar?*"

I pulled a sad face. "Think of all the commissions you'll lose."

"Alex, that's not what this is about."

"Then maybe I'll become an astronaut. Or a garbage man." I reached for his wineglass. He snatched it away, splashing wine on the tablecloth.

"You want to waste your time playing basketball with your juvenile delinquent friends? Fine. Throw your talent away."

"The only talent you seem interested in is how well I spread my legs."

His eyes darted around the room. "You know that's not true," he said, *sotto voce*.

I got up. "I'm leaving."

"Sit down," he ordered softly, grabbing my arm so tight that the pain forced me back into the seat. When he let go, I burst into tears. I sounded like a six-year-old who just lost his first competition. Now everyone was staring. He took me outside, waited until I quieted down, then had his driver take me back to Juilliard.

Later that week I came home to find my parents talking to a man I didn't recognize. At first I thought it had to do with me skipping school. "Alex," he said, extending his hand, "I'm Detective Wilke with the New York City Police Department. I'm here to investigate charges made against your manager." My parents sat frozen

and silent, staring into the distance. "How have you two been getting along?"

"Fine."

"Has he ever done anything improper? Touched you in any
way?"

"No, of course not!" I spat out. "Who said that?"

"The family of another boy has accused him of a very serious
crime."

I was floored. Of course I had assumed I was the only one.
"Who?"

"I'm afraid I can't tell you that."

I had seen a cellist, maybe sixteen or seventeen, leaving his office
once. "He's older than me, right?"

"Actually, a few years younger." I thought of the boys he repre-
sented; there was no one younger. Then I remembered an eleven-
year-old piano prodigy he had recently signed. It was a brick in the
face. "Alex, if he did anything to you, you need to tell me. It's important."

I was repulsed, enraged, and, of all things, jealous. But I wasn't
about to give him up. "I told you, nothing happened."

"Do you think he's capable of something like this?"

Adults ask such stupid questions. "How would I know?" I stood
up. "Can I go now?"

If he answered, I didn't hear him.

I stayed in bed for the next few days. Eventually my father took
me to the family doctor. He couldn't find anything wrong and ad-
vised my parents to send me to a shrink. They refused, preferring to
drag me from bed every morning and drive me to school. Some
days I'd sit through my classes, other days I'd skip out after
homeroom. All I could think about was where *he* was and what was
happening to him. There was no one I could talk to about it without raising suspicion. Then I heard he had gone to prison. I was
shocked. I didn't think people like him went to prison. Part of me
felt sorry for him, but another part was glad. It wasn't right to do
that kind of thing to an eleven-year-old. Everyone talked about

how stupid the boy's parents were for not settling it privately. After that, no one would have anything to do with the kid. Maybe he became an astronaut, or a garbage man.

◢◣◢

As I was no longer studying or practicing, I spent my free time working in a grocery store. Mostly I unpacked boxes and stocked shelves, but occasionally I made deliveries. One day I was sent to an apartment building I hadn't been to before. I was greeted upstairs by a guy of about forty, slightly balding and a little overweight. He waved me inside. I placed the groceries on the table. "You carried these heavy bags by yourself? You must have strong arms." He playfully squeezed my shoulder. "Why don't you sit down a minute and relax?"

Could this guy be any more obvious? "I gotta get back."

"Then stop by later, for a beer or something." He extended a sweaty palm. "I'm Alan."

"Rick." It was the first name that came to mind. "You have to pay me." He looked startled. "For the groceries."

"Oh, sorry." He handed me a pile of bills, and slipped in an extra twenty.

I did go back that evening. We drank beer and watched TV. He tried to kiss me. I pulled away. I had only been kissed once, by *him* that first time. I had no interest in repeating the experience.

"Why are you here, then?"

I got up and walked toward the bedroom. When I reached the door, I turned to find him still on the sofa. "Well," I said, losing my patience, "are we going to do it or not?"

That first evening pretty much characterized our relationship. The sex was no frills, although, unlike *him,* Alan tried to get me off.

I wouldn't let him, though. I wasn't ready to give that kind of control to anybody. I only allowed myself pleasure when I was alone.
And at those times I didn't think about Alan or *him*. I thought
about other men—men without faces.

~~~

"Why do you hate me so much?" Alan asked once after sex.
"I don't hate you." The darkness of the room was peaceful. I
wished he'd shut up.
He snapped on the table lamp. "So what's this about? You come
here for sex, then make me practically rape you." I could feel him
staring at me, waiting for a response.
"Shut off the light, Alan."
And he did.

~~~

I arrived at his building uninvited, in a foul mood after fighting
the icy wind. I stood in the lobby, rubbing my arms and knocking
the dirty snow from my sneakers, waiting for the doorman to wave
me up. Alone in the elevator, I looked up at the mirrored ceiling
and stuck out my tongue. I wondered if I was good-looking. I wondered if it mattered.
Alan was not pleased when he opened the door. I walked past
him, mumbling an obligatory hello, went into the bedroom, un-
dressed, and lay down on the bed. He stood in the doorway, staring
at me. "You know, for awhile I actually thought we could have
something. Now I realize what an idiot I was."
"You're boring me."
He continued, ignoring my comment. "It's been more than a
month, and I don't even know your last name."
"You don't even know my real *first* name."
His face grew so red I thought he was going to burst a blood ves-
sel. "This is all a big joke to you, isn't it? Well I'm putting an end to

it now, while I still have some self-respect." I made a show of chewing a hangnail. "Goddamnit, I'm trying to say something here!"

"Then fucking say it."

He picked up my clothes and threw them at me. "Get out!"

I smiled at him insincerely while playing with one of my nipples. "Come on, Alan, you don't really want me to leave, do you?" He hesitated, trying to fight his lust. He was so weak, and there was nothing I hated more in a man. I despised him as he entered me. Yet every thrust made it increasingly clear how much power I could have over someone. After he climaxed I whispered his name lovingly and pulled him close, like I was going to kiss him. Then I spit in his face. For a moment he was stunned. But it was only a moment.

I woke up in the hospital with a concussion, missing teeth, and a broken arm, my bow arm. Until the moment I saw that cast, I thought I didn't care if I ever played the violin again. Now I realized how much a part of my identity it was. My mom and dad were there, looking truly concerned for the first time ever. I asked about my arm, and they assured me it was going to be OK. They said I had been unconscious for two days. An anonymous caller tipped off the hospital to my location in a nearby lot. When they asked what had happened, I concocted a story about a bunch of kids attacking me. I never saw their faces, so there was no point in reporting it. I was released from the hospital a few days later without anyone questioning me further.

I had already missed too much school to advance to the tenth grade, so I was excused for the rest of the year. I couldn't touch my instruments until my arm healed. With nothing to do, I started sleeping during the days and going out in the evenings. I tried the bars but never got past the door. So I hung out in cruisy public places, smoking dope and giving blow jobs when I felt like it.

One night I came in to find my dad still up, watching a baseball game. I dropped down next to him, raw and achy from an earlier sexual encounter. He didn't look at me or say anything for a long time. Then, his eyes still riveted to the screen, he said, "He did do something to you, didn't he?"

We passed the rest of the game in silence.

Cowboys

I was twelve when I learned my parents were thinking about returning to France. Although I was a French citizen, since we moved to the United States when I was two, I always thought of myself as an American. My sisters and brother were all born here. Jeannette came right after we arrived, Simone three years later, and when I was nine, my brother François. We grew up in a small house in Center City Philadelphia. It never occurred to me that we might live anywhere else.

One day I was in the driveway testing out some moves on my skateboard when my dad came home from work, a copy of *Le Monde* folded tightly under his arm. He drove to a special store every day to pick it up, even though by the time he got it, the news was already old.

"*Ça va, mon fils?*" Are things going well? He seemed tired, but in a good mood.

"Yup." I spun around in a circle on the back wheels of my board.

" 'Yup?' *Qu'est-ce que ça veut dire?*" What does that mean? His tone became mildly stern.

I stopped what I was doing. "It means 'yes'—I mean, *ça veut dire 'oui.'* " We were supposed to speak only French at home, but sometimes I got mixed up because my mom didn't care what language we spoke when my dad wasn't around.

"Jean-Philippe," he said wearily, calling me by my full name, "if you are going to speak English, at least speak it properly. Don't use argot."

"*Oui, Papa.*"

He started up the front steps, then stopped suddenly and turned back. "Jean-Philippe, do you like living here?"

That was a weird question. "You mean in this neighborhood?"

"No. This city, this country."

"Of course."

He said, "Good," but it seemed like he had been hoping for a different answer.

After dinner, I sat down alone in the kitchen to finish my homework. We ate on a European schedule, so when dinner was over, my younger sisters and brother had to go straight to bed. I could hear my parents talking in the den, but I wasn't paying attention to what they were saying until they started arguing. I had never heard them fight before, and it bothered me.

"Lucien, *sois sérieux*." Be serious, my mom said. "This is just another one of your brother Émile's crazy ideas. And you know how those turn out."

"This is different," my dad insisted. "This spa was very successful for many years."

"A long time ago maybe. But things change. If this was such a good idea someone else would have done it already."

"That's what you always say. Why do you have to be so discouraging?"

"I know how Émile talks. 'This place is wonderful. Only needs a little work.' Then you get there. *Vieux, démodé, tombé en ruine*." Old, outmoded, in shambles. "*Non, merci*. Besides, Émile has no common sense. Look what he did, fooling around with that married woman, getting her pregnant. Then she wants to keep the baby. What a mess!" At this point I realized my parents must not have known I was still up, because I never got to hear things like this.

"There are worse things he could do, believe me."

"Yes, like getting you involved in this foolish scheme. You were just promoted at the bank. We're finally able to put away a little money. You're going to throw all that away?"

"You know I've always wanted to have my own business."

"Well, Lucien, we don't always get to do what we want. We have four children to think about. They're settled here, they have friends. Jean-Philippe and Jeannette are beginning a new school in the fall, a good private school they worked hard to get into. You can't just uproot everyone and start over in another country."

"Marie-Thérèse." My father sounded offended. "France is not another country, *c'est notre patrie.*" It's our home.

"*Non, mon chéri,*" she responded, her voice softening. "This is our home now."

I slipped quietly down to my bedroom, which was in the basement, so they wouldn't know I had overheard them. I didn't sleep well that night. It seemed like my whole life was up in the air. I thought about talking to my parents but decided to wait. In a few weeks we'd be going to France, like we did every summer. I figured I'd find out then what we were going to do.

◢◣◥

Our first stop in France was the coast of Normandy. Although I was excited about spending ten days at the beach, I was still preoccupied with the thought that we might be moving. As I sat in the hotel lobby, waiting for my parents to check in, I realized I didn't even know where in France we would live if we did move. I assumed near the spa, but where was that—in Tours, where my father's family was? Paris? Lyon? Here in Normandy? At that moment a boy about my age came running down the staircase. A woman called after him, "Armand, *attend!*" but he shot out the door. I thought he hadn't seen me, but seconds later he was at my side, smiling, black curls tumbling in his face. "Come on!" he said and, without waiting for a reply, grabbed my arm to follow him. I turned to my parents to see if it was OK. My father winked and said, "Be back in time for dinner."

Armand and I became instant friends. During the day we explored miles of beaches and bicycled from one seaside town to another. At night we chased each other on the sand under an inky black sky that disappeared into the ocean. Out of breath, we'd collapse, kicking each other's feet in the still-warm sand while listening to the soft whoosh of the waves. I had lots of friends at home, but they weren't like Armand. He got me to do things I had never done before, like steal apples from people's gardens, sneak into grown-up movies, and set lobsters free from their traps. But it was more than that. I felt a strange excitement every time he took my hand or tossed an arm around my shoulder. I didn't know why it felt so good, and I didn't care.

The day before my family was to leave, Armand and I wandered far down the beach. It was getting late, and there was no one around. We found a pier that stretched from the sand into the water and sat beneath it, shivering in our wet bathing suits.

"I'm cold," I said.

"Me too." He paused a moment, then added, "If we put our arms around each other it'll be warmer."

"OK." My heart began to pound.

"We should lie down," he suggested. So we did. He pressed his small body against mine. I realized, to my embarrassment, that I was getting an erection. This had happened before, when I was alone, but never with another person. I tried to move away, but he tightened his grip. It was now obvious he was in the same condition I was. I looked at him in bewilderment, not knowing what to do. He smiled a funny smile. "Do you want to kiss me?" I nodded apprehensively, afraid that at any moment he was going to laugh and say it was a joke. But he didn't. He moved his face close to mine until our lips touched. I wasn't sure if I was supposed to open my mouth or not. I had never kissed before. "Here, let me show you." He opened my lips with his tongue, warming my whole body.

"Let me try." I did the same.

We kissed for a long time while our hands explored each other's bodies. Looking back, those caresses were achingly innocent. Yet they engendered a happiness in me unlike anything I'd experienced. I felt a whole new world opening up, filled with the promise of pleasure, and of something more, something I was too young to fully understand but knew would be waiting for me when I was ready.

It had gotten dark and cold. I knew we should go home, but I didn't want to stop what we were doing. Eventually Armand jumped up and, challenging me to a race, tore off in the direction we had come. When we were halfway back to the hotel, we saw a distant, moving light. It was my father, flashlight in hand. He gave me an affectionate scolding, then hugged me and said he was glad I was safe.

I said good-bye to Armand the next morning. He gave me a French farewell, brushing his lips against both of my cheeks. On the second kiss he lingered and whispered in my ear, *"Bonne chance."* When he pulled away, I looked into his dark eyes. *"A la prochaine,"* I said, although I knew I would never see him again. He must have known, too, because his smile was sad. We wrote each other a few times but eventually lost touch. I remember him from time to time and hope, wherever he is, he is happy.

~~~

After we left the coast, we visited my mother's parents near Rouen, then drove to Tours, where my father's parents still lived in the house where my father, and I, was born. The day we arrived, Uncle Émile came over. After dinner, he and my dad went off to a little room my grandfather called his "study." There weren't any books in it—just a phonograph and some records. I snuck away from the rest of the family as soon as I could and headed there. Music was coming from the room. My father was always playing French albums at home, and he gave fifty cents to whoever of us could guess the singer. I was pretty good at the game, but I had no idea who this singer was. The recording sounded very old.

I looked into the room. My dad and uncle were sitting at a square table covered with a funny-looking map. There were a couple of empty bottles of wine on the table, and my uncle was opening a third. My dad saw me in the doorway. *"Viens ici,* Jean-Philippe. I want to show you something." I walked over to where he sat. He put his arm around me and gestured to the map. "This is a plan of a spa your uncle is thinking of buying. Don't let your mother know I told you, but we might go in on it too." I waited for him to say more about that, but he didn't. Instead, he pointed to a rectangular box on the map. "Here's the hotel. There's a hundred guest rooms, two dining rooms, and a ballroom."

"Why is there a ballroom in a spa?" I asked.

"Spas are different here than in America—they are more like resorts. People come to take in the waters for their health, but they also like to have fun."

"What are the 'waters'?"

"The spring. Here." His hand circled another part of the page. *"Voila la source.* The whole place will have to be renovated, of course, but what do you think?"

I didn't know what to say. It was hard to tell anything from the map. "It's very interesting."

My father laughed. "Very interesting! Well, we'll see. Maybe this time your uncle Émile has found something." My dad lifted his glass in a toast to Émile and finished off his wine.

"How can you sit there and drink without offering any to your son?" Émile asked disapprovingly. He filled his own glass to the rim and passed it to me.

"No, *c'est trop.*" It's too much, my father protested. "His mother will have a fit." My uncle responded with a vulgar expression I had heard a few times before. I didn't understand what it meant, but I knew it was an insult. I expected my dad to get angry, but all he did was direct me to "drink half, no more." I could tell he was too drunk to pay attention, so I finished the entire glass before slipping off to bed.

The next morning, Émile and Dad took off for Périgueux, which was a few hours away. My mom said they were visiting friends, but I knew they were going to look at the spa. My dad was in great spirits when they left, beeping the car horn and waving to us as they drove away. On their return, though, he walked across the lawn past me and my sisters, like he didn't see us. When my mom greeted him at the door, he said in a heavy voice, *"Vraiment, tu avais raison."* You were right. He had a look on his face that I had never seen before. It was more than disappointment. It was like he had failed at something, or something had failed him. Maybe he continued to dream about moving back to France and running his own business, but I never heard him talk about it again.

᭜᭜

That fall I started junior high. Although it was a new school, I made friends quickly. Nevertheless, that year, and the ones that followed, was difficult as I grew more aware of my sexuality. Not that I had a problem with it. To me, liking guys was as normal as eating and sleeping. Fortunately, my school adhered to the tolerant values of the Quakers who founded it, so I was rarely exposed to the hatred most adolescents express toward homosexuals. Still, I had to be careful. I came out in the beginning of eleventh grade to two female friends, who were fine with it. Then I told a male friend who I thought might be gay too. Unfortunately, I was wrong, or at least that's what he said. Within days he'd told the entire class. Mostly it was whispering behind my back, but one day when I was at my locker, a senior I barely knew stood behind me chanting "cocksucker" over and over. Other guys gathered around, and I panicked, worried they were going to gang up on me. Without thinking, I took a swing at the guy who started it. I landed a punch to his chin, knocking him to the ground. A teacher saw it and reported me to the dean. It was worth it, though. No one bothered me after that.

When I got home, I told my parents what had happened, leaving out the particulars. My mother looked me over frantically. *"T'es tu fait mal?"* Are you hurt?

"He's fine," my father beamed, patting me on the shoulder. "It's the other guy who's not feeling so good, eh?" It was nice seeing him proud of me, although I wondered how he would feel if he knew what the guy had called me, and that it was true. My dad walked over to the liquor cabinet and filled two cognac glasses. "This is why I show you how to defend yourself. But never start a fight, *tu comprends?* You only use it if you have to." He placed one of the glasses in my hand. "This is to celebrate your becoming a man. *Mon fils est devenu homme!*"

I was becoming a man in other ways as well. Because of the gossip about me at school, I received some subtle and not so subtle come-ons from a number of male classmates. At one party, a guy from the football team came up and leaned against me, acting drunk, but it seemed exaggerated, like the way people act in movies. "This party stinks," he said with a goofy smile, his face inches from mine. "I've got some great weed. Want to go to the garage and smoke some?" I agreed but was cautious. I knew something was up. I just hoped it was a good something. As soon as we got into the garage, he pushed me against the wall, fell to his knees, and tore open my pants. I was caught by surprise, but I wasn't complaining. It was my first blow job, and it felt great! Just as things were getting going, though, there was a sound from the other side of the garage door. It was no big deal, but he freaked out and ran. I tried to talk to him the next day at school, but he didn't even want to be seen with me. I tried to tell myself I didn't care. After all, it wasn't like we were friends. Still, it made me feel pretty shitty.

After that I hooked up with a few other guys, but those brief, clumsy encounters only left me disappointed. I was beginning to wonder if I would ever realize the promise I had glimpsed all those years back with Armand.

That spring a neighborhood friend invited me to a party given by his older sister. By the time we arrived, her apartment was packed. I felt conspicuously out of place, as we were much younger than everyone else there. My friend grabbed a couple of beers for us. "You want to meet my sister, Allison?" he asked as he washed down a mouthful of potato chips.

"I want to leave," I grumbled.

"Come on." I followed him because my only other choice was to stand by myself looking stupid. We went into the crowded kitchen. He pointed out his sister, a slim woman of about twenty-five, wearing a sleeveless black dress with a high neck and a low back. Her hair was pulled tightly away from her face and held with a black

velvet bow. Her makeup was vivid, but not overdone. She was attractive, but not beautiful, and there was a hardness in her eyes that
made me think she knew it. My friend introduced us, then promptly
disappeared. "Do you go to school with Joe?" Allison asked, sip-
ping what looked like champagne from a fluted glass.

"No." I told her the name of my high school.

"You're kidding. I went there too! Does Mr. Vesperi still teach
European history?" I nodded. "Does he still wear that awful tou-
pee?"

I laughed. "Yeah."

"When I was a senior, Vesperi was helping Mrs. Marshall, the
drama coach, in a production of *The Crucible*. Everybody said they
were having an affair, but I always thought he had the hots for Miss
Gramble, the librarian. Anyway, one day during rehearsal his tou-
pee got snagged on a piece of scenery, and it went flying across the
stage . . ." I listened attentively to that story, and the next, but
eventually my attention wandered. I noticed a man standing a few
yards behind her, in conversation with another man and a woman.
He was a big, muscular guy, in his late twenties, with light-brown
hair and clean-cut features. I glanced briefly away from him, and
when I looked back, our eyes met. I took a hurried sip of my beer
and returned my gaze to Allison. "So," she said, "did you leave your
girlfriend at home tonight?"

"Huh? Oh, I don't have a girlfriend."

She smiled provocatively and ran her finger down the side of her
champagne glass. "We'll certainly have to do something about
that."

Uh-oh, I thought, and quickly excused myself to the bathroom. I
hoped when I returned she would be occupied with someone else.
When I came out, I was unnerved to see her talking with the guy I
had been staring at. Since they were standing by the kitchen exit,
I had no choice but to try to slip past them. It didn't work. Allison
grabbed my arm and held me there, without introducing me, as she
continued an amusing story about raccoons invading her parents'
home.

When she stopped for a breath, he broke in, his voice piercing the surrounding din with a deep Texas drawl. "I'm Daniel." He smiled warmly and extended his hand.

I said something inane like, "Nice to meet you," and held out my hand to meet his. He gripped it with such force my knees nearly buckled, and a terrible wave of desire racked my body. I was desperate to let him know I was interested, but he left before I could figure out how.

Disappointed, I saw no point in staying. I said good night to Allison, but she refused to let me go and kept me by her side as she chatted with one friend after another. I pretended to listen while I thought about how it would feel to be crushed in Daniel's arms, or to have his massive chest pressing down on mine. Maybe when I got home I'd hug the refrigerator or lie down with the TV on top of me, just to see.

As the night dragged on I got drunk enough to have a good time. I even danced with Allison a few times. Somehow I ended up being the last person there. I was looking through the wreckage for my jacket when I heard her say, in a silly voice I guess was supposed to be sexy, "Why don't you stay tonight?"

"Thanks, but I need to get—" Before I could finish my sentence, she was kissing me. We had sex on the living room floor. Afterward, I could feel her arms around my neck, as heavy as cement boots on a drowning man. I peeled them off and got up.

"What's the matter?"

"I need to go," I said, pulling on my pants.

"Please don't." She rose to her feet. She was thin, with small breasts and protruding hipbones. It was the first time I had seen a woman fully nude, except of course in magazines. I finished dressing. "Fine, go," she said dismissively, walking into the kitchen and lighting a cigarette on the stove. I wondered if another guy would find this a turn-on, seeing a woman walking around naked. I started to imagine Daniel in her place but stopped quickly. If I got another erection she'd never let me go.

When I got home I crawled into bed, trying to forget about what I had done with Allison, thinking instead about what I wanted to do with Daniel. She phoned the next day, apologized for being cross, and asked to see me again. Although I had no real desire for her, it was hard to turn down free sex. It was easier after the first time. At least I knew I could do it. I always thought about Daniel, though. It wasn't that I imagined I was having sex with him. That would have been impossible. It was more that she reminded me of my desire for him. I knew it was wrong to use her that way, but I felt like she was using me too.

After we had been seeing each other for about a month, Allison took me to a restaurant on Twelfth Street between Locust and Walnut, in the heart of the gay section of Center City. Our waiter was about my age and cute, if a bit too blond. He came by repeatedly, and I noticed him looking at me each time. When Allison went to the ladies' room, he appeared again. "Your sister?" he asked.

"Yes," I answered quickly, happy he had supplied the excuse.

"I figured." He smiled flirtatiously. "So, I don't remember seeing you here before."

"It's my first time."

"Next time, ask for me." He reached into his pocket and pulled out a card with the restaurant's name on it. He flipped it over, wrote down his name and phone number, and tossed it on the table. "See you later." He left with a grin. He knew I would call, and I did, the next day. We met, went to a movie and then to his apartment. We sat in the living room with his roommates for awhile, listening to some music, went to his room and had sex. It was like a dam breaking inside of me. When I got home that night, exhausted and happy, there was a note from my mom on the corkboard saying Allison had called. I told myself I should return the call, and the ones that followed, but I didn't. I simply didn't know what to say.

I saw the waiter every night for two weeks. Physically it was great, but we had nothing in common. One evening I asked why we had to spend so much time hanging out with his roommates. He accused me of being with him only for the sex, which was true, although I denied it. That was the last time we saw each other.

A few days passed and I phoned Allison. I apologized for not returning her calls, saying I had been sick. She must have known it was a lie, but she still agreed to see me. After being with the waiter, sex with Allison was more difficult and even less satisfying. But I enjoyed her company. She was intelligent and witty, even if she talked too much.

One day I went to the advertising firm where Allison worked to meet her for lunch. When I arrived, the receptionist told me she was in a meeting and could be tied up for some time. Not willing to wait, I turned to leave. At that moment the elevator dinged and out walked Daniel, the hunky guy from Allison's party. We were both surprised.

"You're . . ." He faltered, offering his hand.

"Philip." I extended my hand to meet his, anticipating the pleasant shock I would receive. I was not disappointed. "And you're Daniel."

He laughed in his warm baritone. "You have a good memory."

Only when I want to, I thought. "You work here?"

"My office is down the hall from Allison's. Are you here to see her?"

"I was going to, but she's busy."

"My lunch date canceled too. I still have reservations if you'd like to join me."

We had lunch on the second floor of a small, sunny café. I was nervous when we sat down, but Daniel's easygoing manner helped me relax. My eyes were lingering a bit too long on his chest, but I had it under control until he removed his blazer and rolled up his sleeves. His white dress shirt molded to the muscles of his upper arms. His lower arms, bare but for a cloak of golden brown hair, hinted gloriously at what was to come. Realizing I was staring, I glanced back up to Daniel's face. He was smiling broadly. I blushed and lowered my eyes to the table.

"So," he said in an easy tone, "how long have you known Allison?"

"Only since the party, where I met you." I lifted my eyes cautiously back to his.

"Are you two romantically involved?" He stretched his elbow casually over the back of his chair.

I gave him a quizzical look. "Of course not."

"That's interesting. She gave me the impression you were."

I shook my head. "She's not my type. Really not my type."

"What is your type?" he asked. I looked into his eyes for an extended moment, hoping he'd understand. Finally he smiled and said, "Why don't we order lunch?"

Daniel took the rest of the day off. I was free, too, as the school year had ended and I hadn't started my summer job yet. We went to the Franklin Institute. Even though I lived nearby, I hadn't been there since grade school. By the time Daniel and I got to the main attraction, a giant replica of a beating human heart, the schoolchildren who typically thronged the exhibit were gone. We entered through one of the two narrow passageways that served as the heart's ventricles. I was keenly aware of the closeness of Daniel's body as he followed me through the tiny chambers, the walls pulsating with increasing intensity as we neared the center.

Afterward we went to his place, a small, newly constructed house not far from my family's. The rooms were bright, with simple, modern furniture. Daniel sat me down on the couch and brought me a beer. Before handing it to me, he said, with mock seriousness, "You are twenty-one, aren't you?"

He knew I couldn't be twenty-one. "You're kidding, right?"

"Of course." He laughed, handing me the beer. "Uh, how old are you, exactly?"

"Eighteen." I had already decided this was what I would tell him if he asked. I was really seventeen.

"You're sure now?"

"I'm sure."

Daniel crossed the room to the unit that housed his sound system. He flipped through a stack of cassettes while unknotting his tie and kicking off his shoes. He popped in a tape and fiddled with the buttons, his legs shifting back and forth in his khakis. Every movement he made was erotic to me. I could hear my blood pulsing, as loud as that giant beating heart.

I was surprised that the music he had chosen was country-western. I had never actually heard that kind of music before, except in snippets used to sell "The Best of . . ." albums of country singers on late-night TV. I made a joke about it being "cowboy" music. "Cowboy music for us cowboys," Daniel responded with a grin. I wasn't sure what that meant, but I liked the way it sounded.

We talked for a long time, but Daniel didn't make a move toward me. "It's getting late," I said finally. "I don't want to take up your whole evening." I got up like I was leaving, but with obvious hesitation.

"You're welcome to stay, Philip, as long as you want." He looked at me as if trying to gauge my reaction.

"OK." I smiled awkwardly and asked to use his phone. I called my parents and told them I would be staying at a friend's. They never gave me any trouble about that, contrary to what I had told Allison to avoid staying at her place. I returned to where I had been sitting next to Daniel on the couch. Very matter-of-factly, he reached past me to switch off the lamp. Then he kissed me. His hand fell to my hip, and he pressed me closer for a longer kiss. My shyness dissipated. I unbuttoned his shirt and slid my hands over his chest. It was solid like the side of a mountain. I tried to tug off his shirt but couldn't because his arms were around me. He saw me struggling and slipped it off himself. I glided my fingers over the biceps that had been part of my fantasies for so long. I could tell he was watching me with amusement. I felt myself blushing again and was thankful for the darkness. As he pulled off my T-shirt, his fingertips brushed my stomach, sending a shiver through me. Slowly, he lowered me onto the couch, and I waited with delicious fear for the weight of his body to descend on mine.

I lost my virginity to Daniel that night. When I woke up the next morning, I was in love and I was scared. I knew the chances of him loving me were next to none. He had told me the night before about his recent split with his lover and hinted that it might not be permanent. It was clearly his way of telling me not to get too emotionally involved. But that was impossible. That first night created a permanent connection between us, in my mind anyway.

I broke it off with Allison the next day. I made the mistake of doing it in person, at her apartment. I knew I was in trouble when I came in to dim lighting and mood music. I had to get to the point fast, or she would pounce. "Allison," I said as she sat down too close to me, "I wanted to tell you . . . I'm seeing someone else."

"What?"

I knew I couldn't tell her it was Daniel. "It's not anybody you know." I paused and, in a burst of naive frankness, added, "It's a guy."

She stood up, her eyes blazing. "You're a fucking liar. You're only saying that to hurt me."

"No, I'm telling you so you'll know it has nothing to do with you."

"You've cheated on me this entire time, haven't you?"

"No, no," I assured her. "I wouldn't do that. That's why I'm telling you now."

She grabbed her cigarette pack from the coffee table, hands trembling. "Please don't do this," she said softly.

"I'm sorry." I took a step toward the door, but she rushed to get there before me, blocking my escape. I was trapped for what seemed like hours, listening mutely as she hurled strings of insults and accusations at me. Finally, her voice hoarse, she stepped aside. I left with a feeling of freedom, but also of loss. She had been a good friend.

I settled down as best I could in my relationship with Daniel. I had a great time when we were together, but as the summer passed, those times were becoming increasingly rare. One Thursday in early August I called to ask when we could see each other. He said he was busy the entire weekend. I knew this was a bad sign, but I didn't know what to do about it.

The next evening I was setting the table for dinner when the phone rang. I picked it up, thinking it was Dad saying he was leaving the office. But it was a woman, calling from the hospital. My father had had a heart attack and was in intensive care. It seemed impossible. He was only forty-four. He smoked a lot and was overweight, but I didn't remember him being sick a day in his life. After dropping off my youngest sister and brother with a neighbor, my mom drove with Jeannette and me to the hospital. I'd never seen her so afraid. We spent the entire night there. By early morning the doctor assured us my father was stabilized and recommended we go home. As my mother turned the key in the front door, we heard the phone ringing. She rushed in to pick it up, was silent for a moment, then began screaming.

The minute we entered the hospital room I was struck by how empty it felt. There was no one there, certainly not my father. My mother moved cautiously to the bed, looking at the body that lay there like she wasn't sure whose it was. She sat next to it and cried. I watched, numb, like all this was happening to someone else. In the background was the drone of daily life, phones ringing, people talking, the bells and buzzers of a game show on TV. The sounds mixed together and became louder and louder until they were unbearable. I ran from the room. Jeannette called after me, but I couldn't stop.

I ran until I found myself at Daniel's door. I didn't know how I had gotten there. I knocked. No one answered. I rang the bell. Still nothing. I pressed down on the buzzer again and again, feeling more frantic as the seconds passed. Finally Daniel threw open the door, agitated, holding his bathrobe closed with one hand. Our eyes met, and his expression changed.

"Philip, what are you doing here? It's eight o'clock in the morning." He paused and took a closer look at me. "God, you look awful. What's the matter?"

"I had to see you," I said, out of breath.

"But I told you we couldn't see each other this weekend." He was kind but firm.

"I know." I closed my eyes painfully. "Please let me in, just for a minute."

"I can't, Philip." I looked at him, bewildered. He shook his head wearily. "You've put me in a very difficult position."

Suddenly, I understood. "Someone's there with you. Another guy?" His silence provided the answer. "Excuse me for interrupting." I turned away sharply. He grasped my arm.

"I'm sorry, Philip," he said gently. "Call me later and we'll talk." I yanked away and broke into a fresh run. I ran without knowing where I was going. I ran through red lights and oncoming traffic. I crashed into people on the sidewalk. I tripped and fell without feeling anything. Eventually I couldn't go any farther. I leaned against a building, panting and holding my side. My father was wrong when he said I had become a man the day I threw my first punch. And I was wrong when I thought I'd lost my innocence the first time I felt the pressure of Daniel's body in mine. No, it was all happening now, as I stood doubled over in an empty lot, fighting to catch my breath.

◆◆◆

Until my grandparents flew in late Sunday, Jeannette and I were in charge. My mother wouldn't leave her room—not even to wash or eat. I had never seen her like this, and it made me scared. I think Jeannette was scared, too, but we pretended we weren't because we needed to keep calm for Simone and François. Telling them about my father was the worst, especially François. He was too young to really understand and kept asking if I was sure. Sometimes I caught François looking toward the door, as if he expected Dad to be walking through it any moment, laughing and carrying a bag of dime-store chocolates. It happened to me once, too, when I saw a man's legs descending the staircase from the second floor. For an instant, I simply forgot Dad was gone. I almost burst out crying when I saw it was Uncle Émile, but I stopped myself. I had made a decision not to cry, afraid that, like Mom, I wouldn't be able to stop.

I don't remember anything about the funeral except the stifling heat. I was almost thankful for it. It made it virtually impossible to think about anything else. At the cemetery, my mother comforted me for the first time. As she circled me in her arms, I saw Daniel coming toward us. When our eyes met, I turned away, leaning on my mom for support. I wasn't ready to face him. When I looked up again, he was gone.

Three weeks passed before I called him. When I came to his door it sent me right back to that awful day. I thought about leaving but braced myself and knocked. He opened the door and led me in. "I'm glad you're here."

"Sorry I couldn't speak to you at the funeral."

He dropped his hand on my shoulder. "Completely understandable."

"How did you find out?"

"I saw the obituary."

"You read the obituaries? Why?"

"For the same reason I tell you to use a condom *every time*." I swallowed hard and nodded. It was difficult enough being faced with my father's death. I wasn't ready to contemplate my own.

We sat on the couch. He took my hands in his. "Listen, I want to explain about that day."

I lowered my eyes. "You don't have to."

"I've always been honest with you, Philip. I told you about Bob from the beginning because I had a feeling we might get back together, and we did. I never wanted to hurt you. I care about you very much. Actually, I love you."

It was the first time he had said that. I can't imagine the expression on my face. "You're really confusing me."

"I know. I'm sorry." He paused, seeming to struggle for the right words. "You're too young for me. I'm too old for you. It's that simple."

I pulled back from him. "That's discrimination."

He took a deep breath, trying to suppress a smile at my silly indignation. "No. It's an understanding of the way things are."

I felt like he was patronizing me. I stood up. "I don't want to hear any more."

"Philip, this is the last time we're going to see each other. Please listen to what I have to say." I stopped and stood by the couch as he continued to speak, my face turned away. "It's not only the age difference. I'm still in love with Bob. I could keep seeing you. Bob wouldn't even care. But you deserve better than that. You deserve someone who's focused exclusively on you, and right now I'm not that person."

I thought about storming out in a huff, but that seemed infantile. Anyway, it wasn't what I wanted. "Daniel, could you do me a favor?"

"Anything."

"Let me stay with you tonight?"

He smiled gently. "That's hardly a favor."

Upstairs, as we were undressing, I began to cry quietly. I felt his big hand cradling the back of my head. "Can we just talk awhile?" I asked. So we lay in bed and talked, or rather I talked and he listened. I told him about a lot of things I remembered from when I was a kid, things about my dad. I knew it didn't mean anything to him, but it was nice telling somebody. And I talked about that day, the day he died, and how it felt. I must have fallen asleep after that, because I don't remember anything more.

We made love in silence the next morning. What a relief not to talk, not to think. It was almost noon by the time I got up. As I finished tying the laces of my sneakers, he reached out and pulled me close to him. We kissed softly. I waved once at his bedroom door and was gone.

Le Petit Prince

I first met Alex after a high-school recital in the fall of my senior year. Those of us who were not musically inclined tended to doze through these things, but when Alex played, I woke up. My attention, I'll have to admit, was attracted as much by his sullen good looks as his musical abilities. He played Bach's Concerto in D Minor. It was supposed to be for two violins, but he had arranged it for solo violin and piano, probably because there wasn't another violinist in the school willing to share the stage with him. He played with ferocious energy, keeping every note tightly within his control.

When the recital was over, I went backstage to find my sister Jeannette, who had played as well. People were milling about, packing up their instruments. I saw the violinist standing alone, looking bored and distracted. "Isn't he in your class?" I asked Jeannette, gesturing in his direction.

"Alex? Used to be. He's repeating ninth grade." She tucked her flute into its velvet case and clicked the metal buckles closed.

"Why was he held back?"

She looked up, tossing her mane of orange-red hair out of her face. "Supposedly he had some kind of accident, but I think it's because he cut class all the time."

"Introduce me."

She screwed up her face. "Why would you want to meet *him?* He's weird."

I grabbed her arm and dragged her over. He was facing the wall now, putting away his violin. Jeannette called his name. He turned around slowly, clearly displeased at having been disturbed.

"This is my brother, Philip," Jeannette grumbled. "He wanted to meet you for some reason."

As Alex looked at me, his expression softened. "Hi," he said in an unassuming voice, with a slight arch to one eyebrow.

"Hi," I echoed, then stood tongue-tied, caught in the stare of those wild blue eyes. He blinked, setting me free. I blurted out a string of awkward phrases complimenting his performance. He thanked me graciously, a small smile twitching at his lips. I asked a slew of questions that he must have answered a thousand times before, yet he responded thoughtfully. Perhaps he was only being polite, but I hoped it was something more.

The next day I saw him in the main hall. We exchanged hellos. "You going down?"

He smiled at me blankly. "Down where?"

"To the cafeteria. It's lunch period."

"Oh." He paused. "Sure." He dropped his book bag next to the others lining the walls. "You want to eat in the graveyard?" he asked.

It was too cold outside for that, but I agreed anyway. We got coffee from the cafeteria and headed out. The graveyard, which was across a footpath from the main building, was a popular student hangout on warmer days. I got a kick out of telling people we had a cemetery on campus, but it was really more like a small park. It was connected to a Friends' Meetinghouse, the Quaker equivalent of a church, which shared the school grounds. The graveyard had not been in use for over a century, and its few dozen gravestones dated back to the 1800s.

Alex dropped down under a giant elm and tore the plastic lid from his coffee cup. I sat on one of the squat headstones and opened my lunch. "Aren't you eating?" I asked.

"This is it." He raised his coffee cup and took a gulp.

I held out half my sandwich. He waved it away. "Boeuf Bourguignon, from last night's dinner. You don't know what you're missing."

He took it hesitantly. "Well, maybe a bite."

Contrary to what Jeannette had told me, Alex was not weird. It's true he wasn't like other kids. He didn't know anything about rock groups, or movies, or even what was on TV. But that was because he practiced the violin for five hours a day. It sounded boring to me, but he said he didn't mind. Besides, he got to do a lot of things and go places other kids never did. He had played with orchestras all over the country, and in Europe, and had won a bunch of competitions. He didn't brag about it—it was like normal life to him. I liked hearing about where he had been and the people he'd met. I liked looking at him, too. He had a kind of gawky grace, like that rhyme about boys being all frogs and snails and puppy dog tails. His fingernails were ragged, his neck needed a wash, and he ate like a savage. But there was refinement in him, like an impoverished aristocrat—one who had been raised by wolves. He had a expression that seemed to say, "I know what you're thinking, but I won't tell." I wondered if he knew what I was thinking.

We ate lunch together nearly every day and spent all of our free periods together. Every Thursday morning we sat side by side in the Meetinghouse, a large, plain room filled with row upon row of dark wooden pews. There were no altars, paintings, sculptures, or stained glass. The walls were two stories high, lined with enormous windows. Sunlight streamed in, illuminating elongated rectangles of floating dust. There was a sense of serenity, all the more profound due to the absence of sound. Quakers do not have a service. Meeting for Worship is conducted in silence, except for those occasions when someone is "moved by the spirit" to share their thoughts. Unlike the more traditional service my parents, now my mom, dragged us to a few times a year, I occasionally had spiritual thoughts during Meeting. Nevertheless, when left to think in silence for forty-five minutes, my thoughts were more likely to drift to the sexual than the spiritual. This was especially true with Alex sitting nearly flush against me in a crowded pew.

Alex and I tried to see each other outside of school as well, but it was hard. He had music lessons three afternoons a week, shrink appointments on the other two. The rest of the time he was practicing. I was busy, too, with soccer in the fall and basketball in the winter. Fortunately, we lived only a few blocks apart, so Alex dropped by sometimes in the evenings. We'd sit in the kitchen, drink coffee, and talk. Sometimes my mom joined us, tempting Alex with leftovers from dinner. He usually made a mild attempt at protest, then pounced on whatever was put in front of him. Alex charmed my mom, complimenting her cooking and appearance, and asking her opinion on everything from the future of the common market to French opera singers. She extended him an open-ended invitation to dinner. To my surprise, he took her up on it immediately.

The first time Alex ate with us was weird. It was the usual uproar, Simone and François kicking each other under the table, Jeannette refusing to eat something or other because of her diet. In the beginning, Alex seemed overwhelmed. By the end of the meal, though, he was entertaining the whole family with a nonsense song in French. The tune he sang was the famous love duet from the Catherine Deneuve film, *Les Parapluies de Cherbourg*. But the words were of the kind you'd find in a tourist's phrase book. *"Comment allez-vous, parlez-vous anglais? Voici ma femme, òu est Notre-Dame?"* François laughed so hard he spit a pea across the table. Alex seemed to enjoy himself too. When I walked him to the door, he asked, "Why didn't you tell me your real name was Jean-Philippe?"

"Everyone calls me Philip except my family." He gave me an odd look, almost like he was hurt I didn't consider him part of the family. "You can call me Jean-Philippe if you want."

"Nah. Can't even pronounce it. I'll have to come up with my own name for you." He smiled mischievously. "Phil. I'll call you Phil."

"Sounds like an auto mechanic."

"Phil, Phil, Phil," he taunted. I never would have let anyone else call me that, but Alex said it with such teasing affection I almost liked it.

Sometimes I came home from after-school sports to find Alex playing Battleship on the living-room floor with François, helping Simone with her homework, or yakking it up with Jeannette. Without knowing it, Alex filled some of the emptiness left by my father's passing, without in any way replacing him. My feelings for

Alex, though, had nothing to do with my father. I knew I was attracted to him and cared for him a great deal, but I wasn't ready to express it. Part of the problem was that, while I was pretty sure Alex was gay, I didn't know if he knew it. I was also a little afraid of his mood swings. I tried to chalk it up to artistic temperament, but I wondered why he saw a shrink twice a week. Once a week was pretty much de rigueur in our school. More than that meant something was wrong.

I got the answer to some of my questions in the early spring, while we were shooting baskets outside my house. After he'd sunk yet another one, I said, "You could easily make varsity. You should try out next year."

"Next year I'll be at Curtis." He grinned slyly, tossing the ball up into the air.

Curtis was a local music college, thought by many to be the equal of Juilliard. I was impressed. "When did you find out?"

"Today."

I resisted the urge to hug him, afraid it would turn into something neither of us was ready for. "How'd you get them to take you without finishing high school?"

He dribbled the ball around me. "They take students at any age. I still have to get a high school diploma, but I can do it while I'm at Curtis. I wanted to go this year, but it didn't work out."

"Because of the accident?" He stopped dribbling. It was the first time I had brought up the subject with him.

"Accident?" He laughed in a funny way. "I guess you could call it that."

I was nervous about pursuing it, but I knew this might be my only chance. "What happened exactly?"

Alex jumped, shooting the ball over my head. It dropped into the basket, nothing but net. "You sure you want to know?"

I hesitated. "Yeah."

"It's no big deal, really," he said blandly, retrieving the ball. "I used to work at a grocery store. I started screwing around with a guy I made deliveries to. One day we got into a fight, blah, blah, blah, and I was in the hospital for a few days."

"Were you badly hurt?"

"A few broken bones." He leaned against the garage door, cradling the ball. I stared at him, unnerved by his nonchalance. "What's the matter, freaked out because I'm a homo?"

"No," I answered quickly. Figuring now was as good a time as any, I added, "So am I." When he didn't react, I started blathering. "It's just pretty shitty, that's all, beating up a kid. How old was this guy, anyway?"

"I don't know." He stretched his mouth in a yawn. "Forty maybe." My eyes widened. He snorted. "The guy before him was even older."

"You like doing stuff with old guys?" OK, I had been with Daniel, but there's a difference between ten years older and twenty-five years older.

"Sure. Why not?" he asked, his voice turning brittle. "Not that it's your business."

"I'm sorry, I just . . ." I was afraid I would say something else stupid, so I merely repeated, "I'm sorry."

He glared at me for a moment, then threw the ball at my chest. "It's your shot."

〰〰〰

During the following month our relationship remained guarded. Now I knew for sure Alex was gay, but I still wasn't ready to act on my feelings. I was put off by his relationships with older men and the creepy pride he took in them. I also was aware that I was his only friend. If I made a move, he might see it as a betrayal of our friendship. So I tried to maintain things as they were between us, despite the new tension.

Alex was the one who changed things. One afternoon he stopped by a track meet I was competing in. I lost the race, but we had a good time afterward, getting a slice of pizza and playing video games in my room. During the last game, I felt his leg brush up against mine a couple of times. It seemed like an accident, so I ignored it. By the time the game was over, his mood had shifted dramatically. He paced the room, his arms folded across his chest. I couldn't stand it when he got like this. "Let's shoot some baskets," I suggested.

"No."

"How about going to Record World?"

"I don't have any money," he grumbled. "Time for a new sugar daddy."

I sighed. "Why do you make jokes like that?"

"I wasn't joking."

"After what's happened to you, I can't believe you'd want to be with a guy like that again."

"Like you're an improvement."

I shook my head in confusion. "What?"

He walked toward me, stopping only inches from my face. "Why don't you just admit you want to fuck me?" I stared at him, dumbfounded. "Oh," he said with mock sympathy, "I see I've misjudged you. You must be a blow job kind of guy." He laughed, but it was mean. "At least the others were honest about what they wanted from me. At least they weren't hypocrites." I opened my mouth, but before I could say anything, he left. I collapsed on my bed, wondering how this could have happened. I knew it wasn't my fault, but it didn't matter. I was devastated things had ended this way.

The next day Alex was waiting for me outside my last class. He was pale, and the sensuous circles under his eyes were puffier than usual. "Will you talk to me?" he asked meekly once the other students had left.

"Yeah," I mumbled halfheartedly, hurt from what had happened but still glad to see him.

"Yesterday was . . ." He shook his head. "I'm sorry. I don't know why I said what I said."

He looked too pathetic for me to stay angry at him. "It's OK."

"Really?"

"Yeah."

"Listen." He was so nervous he was almost shaking. "There's something I have for you, but you have to come to my house. Will you do that?"

The first floor of Alex's cramped, dark house was like one of those musty rooms in a library used to store odd-sized and rarely requested materials. Dusty bookshelves lined the walls, laden with sheet music thrust between scores of multivolumed texts. A round oak table covered with old newspapers balanced on uneven legs in one corner of the living room. A baby grand piano dominated another. Although the house was less than inviting, I felt comfortable there, amused and inspired by its aggressive lack of order. But I was jittery, too, not knowing what Alex had planned. I watched curiously as he took a guitar from its case.

"I wrote something for you."

"Wow." I was flattered and surprised. Up to this time, I had heard him play only in public concerts, always on the violin, and always works by other composers. This was exciting.

He tuned his guitar, then paused to let silence fill the room before he began. Listening to Alex's music was like wandering in a strange country where the landscape was bleak and majestic, and I was lost and alone. Alex's head was bent while he played, and I couldn't see his face. During certain passages I forgot it was my friend sitting there and instead saw only a composer playing a new work. I felt, for the first time, part of something greater than myself.

After the final note, Alex sat very still, then looked up at me. The composer was gone, and the sixteen-year-old had returned. He was waiting for me to say something, but everything I could think of was fantastically inadequate. "You really wrote that for me?"

He nodded. "I've worked on it for weeks. Couldn't seem to get the end right. Then last night, well, this morning, really . . ." He trailed off, scratching his head. "What do you think?"

"It was the most beautiful thing I've ever heard. And probably the saddest." I waited, mustering my courage. "I wish you didn't have to be so sad."

He looked at me, his eyes reflecting the dim light of the room. He sat upright, elegant in his exhaustion. I thought momentarily of *Le Petit Prince*. When I was a child, more than anything in the world I wanted to be friends with the little prince. I'd lie in bed before falling asleep at night, imagining our adventures as we traveled the universe together.

I leaned forward and, without thinking, swept a lock of hair back from his face. He stood up suddenly. I tensed, prepared for a tantrum, but none followed. Instead, he drew me up in front of him, circled an arm around my waist, and pressed his body against mine, trustingly, like a child. I had never been this close to him before, and I was inundated by the sour-sweet smell of his sweat. I ran my hand up his spine to his long, supple neck. I fingered a cluster of callouses there, a mark of the constant press of the violin. Then I plunged my hand into his tangle of hair. Suddenly, he had me on the couch and was opening all my clothing. I was so transfixed by his touch, I forgot where I was and who I was with. He called my name. I opened my eyes, remembering. Then, in the tenderest voice I had ever heard him use, he asked, "Will you fuck me?"

We were up the stairs and almost to his room when I remembered the long-unused condoms in my knapsack. Daniel had slipped them in there the last time we were together, a surprise going-away present. "Wait a minute," I said to Alex and rushed back down to get them. When I returned, Alex was already in bed. Once I was out of my clothes, he pulled me under the covers and on top of him. I was really nervous. I had never done this before. After allowing me the briefest of moments to fumble with the condom, he pushed me inside of him. I was not there long, though. A wave of pleasure hit me almost instantaneously, and it was over.

The next thing I was aware of was Alex holding my wrist over his face, looking at my watch. "Shit! My mom will be home any second." He leapt up.

"What?" I asked, stupefied, still in that other world.

"Hurry up," he said, dressing rapidly.

"But, but—"

"I'm serious. You have to go."

As I walked the short distance to my house, I was haunted by Alex's restless, brooding music. My time with him had been so short. I tried unsuccessfully to re-create the image of his naked body, which I had glimpsed only briefly, and to recall the feel of his skin. I hadn't even gotten to kiss him. I wanted to run back and make love to him a hundred times. And given Alex's unpredictability, I wondered if I'd ever get the chance to again.

I struggled all evening over whether to call him. I knew I should, but I was afraid of what his reaction might be, afraid he would pretend nothing had happened. "Phil?" he said when he came to the phone, his voice full of sleepy wonder.

"Did I wake you?"

"No." He laughed. "Well, yes. I guess I conked out after you left. Would you believe my mom was like two hours late?"

"That's too bad."

"Yeah."

I had to say something more. "I wish I could have stayed."

There was silence on the other end of the line. When his voice returned it was edgy and intimate. "Maybe tomorrow."

Those early weeks were full of delightful discoveries, the first being teaching Alex how to kiss. Despite the big talk, Alex's sexual experiences were surprisingly limited, and he was almost a virgin to pleasure. The first time I went down on him, he burst into amazed laughter. I laughed too, proud and pleased that I was able to make him so happy.

And so I told Alex I loved him, one night as we lay pressed together in the dark. The words escaped in a whisper, before I realized what I was saying. Silence followed. Then he cleared his throat, said he had to get home, and left abruptly. I felt stupid and hurt. I left a few messages on his phone machine the next week, but he didn't call back. It was summer, so we didn't see each other at school. My misery deepened as the weeks passed. Then one day he showed up at my door, cocky but nervous. "What's up?"

"Where've you been?" I tried to sound like I didn't care, but I couldn't pull it off.

"Hanging out."

"What do you want, Alex?"

"The usual." I started to close the door on him, but he stopped it with his hand. "Come on, Philip. We have a good time together. Let's leave it at that, OK?"

"Whatever you want."

Sex was mechanical, bordering on rough. I didn't kiss him, I didn't hold him, and when it was over, I immediately rolled away. He looked at me like I had run over him with a truck. Part of me was glad. I wanted him to know what it was like. Still, I felt bad when he said, "Please, Phil, don't be like this. Can't we go back to the way it was?" So we did, beginning a pattern that would last many months, during which we were apart almost as much as we were together. Each time we argued, Alex would storm out, saying hateful, appalling things. But he kept coming back, and I kept taking him back.

Then a few months passed without any major incident. Alex was even becoming less cautious in expressing his emotions. One evening I was lying next to him in my bed, blissfully recalling the words he had said to me moments before, when I was deep inside him, words that were as emotionally powerful as they were profoundly erotic. Now, lying in his arms, I knew I was in danger of blurting out another naked confession of love. I searched instead for something simple and affectionate that wouldn't cause him to bolt like he had in the past. Before I had the chance, though, Alex pulled away and, in a voice frightening in its steadiness, said, "I hope you don't believe that crap I say when we fuck." The joy of the afternoon instantly evaporated. "I say that to everyone in bed." He stretched carelessly. "It doesn't mean anything."

I blinked a few times. "Please leave." He pursed his lips, treating my anger like it was something he couldn't possibly take seriously. Then he rose and dressed leisurely. "I don't want to see you again," I said when he was finished.

"Right." He turned to go up the basement stairs.

"Alex, I know you've said the same thing to me many times and haven't meant it. I mean it."

He gave a little nod and left. I cried the entire evening. At dinnertime, my sister Jeannette came down to get me when I didn't respond to my mother's call. Not able to stand her incessant pounding, I threw on some clothes and opened the door. "What is your problem?" she asked testily as I dropped back down to my bed. Then she looked at my face. "I'll tell Mom you're not feeling well," she said, and quickly turned to leave.

"Jeannette, wait. I need to talk to someone." Despite my efforts not to, I started crying again. It was so embarrassing—like she was seeing me naked.

"Did you have a fight with Alex?" she asked gently. I was surprised, and it must have shown, because she said, "Did you think I didn't know about you two?" I nodded. "Get real! He's over here almost every night, and you two are so lovey-dovey it makes me want to barf." I could tell she was trying to make me laugh, but I couldn't even manage a smile.

Jeannette stood over me and patted my shoulder. It was weird having my sister comfort me. "Jean-Philippe, I don't know what happened with Alex, but it's obvious you guys love each other. You should try to work things out."

I shook my head, knowing she was wrong. Alex didn't love me. If he did, he couldn't have said those things.

My mom called down again. *"J'arrive!"* Jeannette yelled, announcing she was on her way and nearly shattering my eardrums in the process. She turned back to me. "I'll come down after dinner, if you want, and we can talk some more." Jeannette listened patiently that night as I went on and on about my troubles with Alex and offered what advice she could. Without her, I don't know how I would have gotten through those next few days.

At the end of the week, Alex called. "I want to see you," he said, as if nothing had happened.

"Too bad." I slammed down the phone. He called back, mildly frantic, and pleaded for the chance to explain in person.

"Of course, I was lying," he began offhandedly, once we were face-to-face in my room. "I never say stuff to other guys in bed."

"You were lying," I repeated numbly. How could I not know that? It was exactly the type of thing Alex would lie about.

"So, there's no reason for you to be upset."

"No reason?" I would have laughed at the absurdity of his statement if I hadn't been so angry. "You make up a lie to hurt my feelings, and I'm not supposed to be upset?" He stiffened at the violence in my voice. I could tell he was scared. Good. "You know what I liked best? How you slipped in that you're seeing other guys. Was that intentional, or an extra bonus?"

"No, I . . ." He seemed confused. "That's not what I meant."

"What's next? Are you going to tell me my cock's too small, or I don't know how to fuck?"

"I would never say something like that."

"Like what you said wasn't just as humiliating."

He averted his eyes. "I only said that because I was afraid."

"What the hell do you have to be afraid of?"

"Of you. Of me. Of what I was feeling. Of what I said." He lowered his voice. "Of what I was about to say. I'm sorry. I really am."

"You keep saying that, but things aren't getting any better." My voice softened as my anger dissipated. "I'm tired of having to hide my feelings, Alex, and tired of you hurting me because you can't deal with yours." He wrapped his arms around his chest, hugging himself. "We need to take a break from each other," I said.

"For how long?"

"I don't know." I had to tell him something. "At least until after finals."

His eyes widened. "But that's more than two months away."

"I have to concentrate on school, and I can't do that with this nonstop drama."

"I won't cause any more scenes, Phil, I promise." I didn't respond. "Can't we at least meet once in a while?" I shook my head gently. "Can I call you?"

This one was harder. "I don't think that's a good idea."

The room got very quiet. "What happens at the end of the two months?"

"I don't know."

He walked away from me, his head lowered. I wanted to stop him, comfort him, but I knew if I did, my resolve would crumble. I was sad but relieved when he left.

During the next few weeks Alex called or came by the house nearly every day. At my request, Jeannette firmly but politely turned him away. I also received three letters from him, which I placed unopened in my dresser. I tried to block all thoughts of him. The hardest time was at night in bed. My mind would overflow with images of him, and of us together. They kept me awake until I stopped fighting them, then they helped me get to sleep.

I got home after my last exam and half expected to see Alex on my doorstep. Then I realized I hadn't heard from him for a month, since I received his last letter. I didn't know if he still wanted to see me. I didn't even know if I wanted to see him. I missed him, but I didn't want to go back to the way things were. I turned to his letters, hoping they would help me decide. They were nothing at all like I had imagined. The first one began, "I feel so naked when you look at me. More than naked. Like I have no skin. And you, peering into my brain, my thoughts, even my soul. That's why I always think you know my true feelings, even when I lie.

"What I said to you that day, I said because I panicked, feeling those words swimming in my mouth. I love you. Those words terrify me. But it terrifies me more to think I may never get to say them to you."

The second envelope contained an erotic billet-doux. "I know when you're going to share that part of yourself with me. You become so shy, so quiet. It's unlike you, yet it is you. I know by the way your back arches when I rub your nipples between my finger and thumb, the way your head rolls back, exposing your strong neck to my eyes and mouth, the silence with which you wrap your legs around me, the way you close your eyes, or keep them open.

"Your body is so much more supple than I expect. It opens up to me. You open up. I never thought a guy like you would desire me that way. I never thought anyone would desire me that way. Funny how you make even that desire seem masculine. But then, there is no pretense with you. You strip everything down to its essentials. And that's what makes you, and our relationship, so exciting."

The final letter was bleak. "I hear your voice in my head sometimes. Mostly I hear you telling me you love me, although it seems so long ago. And your voice is nearly drowned out in my memory by my own deafening heartbeat. It makes me feel so lonely.

"I'm going to stick it out for the remaining time. I'm trying not to have any hope, yet I have some. Whatever your decision, please tell me to my face. I want to see you again, even if it's the last time."

I read the letters twice, then called him. He was at my house within fifteen minutes. When I saw him standing at the back door, like he had so many times before, I wanted to throw my arms around him. But I stopped myself. I didn't want it to happen like that.

"Did you read my letters?" he asked anxiously, once we got down to my room.

"Yeah. Just now." I had so much to say, but every time I looked at him I was bombarded by the details of his appearance, how well his jeans fit, the beauty of the tiny triangle of bare skin exposed by his open collar, the way his clothing, all blue, made his eyes turn the color of the Aegean. Defeated, I collapsed in a chair.

Alex approached timidly. "What's the matter?"

"I had so much I wanted to say, but now everything's all jumbled."

He crouched in front of me. "All I need to hear is one word, yes or no."

I waited a moment. Had I not decided yet? I looked at him. "Yes." I paused to give myself a chance to change my mind, but the same answer came out. "Yes."

He smiled broadly. "You look like you're not sure. But don't worry." He stood up and began to unbutton his shirt absentmindedly, as if now that everything was all right between us, there was no reason for him to remain dressed. "I know I ruined it the last time we were together." The beautiful triangle grew bigger. "It won't happen again." His shirt fell to the floor. He reached for his belt buckle.

I stopped him. "The things you said in your letters, did you mean them?"

"Yes."

"Then say them to me. Now."

He looked down and shifted his weight nervously. His words were soft but certain. "I feel so naked when you look at me. More than naked. Like I have no skin. And you, peering into my brain, my thoughts, even my soul." I pulled him toward me, pressing my face to his abdomen. Closing my eyes, I wondered, which is the greater fool, the man who trusts his faithless lover, or the one who fails to trust his devoted one? And which fool was I?

Overs

The moment Janna opened the door, she knew they were gone. The house was too quiet, like a spellbound kingdom. A set of keys on the hall table anchored a note that merely said, "Thanks, P and A," in Philip's handwriting. She crushed the scrap of paper in her hand and held it there, tightly. She sat at the foot of the stairs, not yet ready to face the empty closets and dressers, the stripped bed, and the absence of all those small things scattered throughout the house that had assured her, during these too-short months, that they were here.

~~~

Philip arrived early and sat down at one of the tables. He had spent too many afternoons in this hole-in-the-wall, its only attraction being its proximity to Curtis. The waitress came around with a menu. He shook his head, requesting only coffee. When it arrived it was so bitter he pushed it away and asked for a glass of water. He stared out of the window, mindlessly watching the passersby. The temperature was pushing the upper fifties, yet it was still gray and overcast, the gloom only occasionally punctuated by a faint ray of sunlight.

After the blow-up at Janna's, it took Philip a few days to track down Alex, who was hiding out in a friend's apartment. Philip apologized over and over for what he had done—for kissing Janna, for hitting him. He pleaded for another chance. Alex eventually gave in but remained wary. Sometimes when Philip touched him, he flinched, as if anticipating another blow. When that happened, Philip felt so despicable that he was unable to bear Alex's presence and would find an excuse to leave. They saw each other less as the weeks passed, and each time was more tense and depressing. They still had sex, but it was a dim reflection of what it used to be.

Philip did not know how to get back to where they had been. He even considered couple therapy but came up with too many reasons not to, including the cost. Besides, it seemed ridiculous for people their age to go to counseling. When you're twenty-one, if a relationship doesn't work, you move on. But Philip couldn't move on. Instead, he took the coward's way out. He cheated on Alex, repeatedly. Each time he felt tremendous relief during the act, followed by crushing guilt and self-reproach. He thought Alex would know just by looking in his eyes, but by this time Alex no longer looked in his eyes. Philip's guilt over his infidelities tore at the already fragile fabric of their relationship. In a way, it was what he wanted, hoping that eventually the wedge between them would be so deep it would split them cleanly apart.

The last time they had been together, Alex had been so listless during sex that Philip couldn't continue. They lay in silence awhile, then Philip drew him into his arms. He knew they were reaching the end. As difficult as the past weeks had been, he still felt his heart breaking. "Will you stay the night, please?" he requested, thinking how strange it was for him to have to ask this of Alex. "Yes," Alex responded, without adding "of course," as Philip had hoped. Sometime during the night they made love, and Philip briefly felt the return of a connection between them. By morning, though, they had retreated to their separate corners and parted with a minimum of words.

Philip looked up to see Alex framed in the doorway of the diner. He was wearing a moth-eaten sweater and tattered jeans. His cheeks were ruddy and he was out of breath. He dropped down across the table from Philip. "Sorry I'm late." Philip waited for Alex to continue, since it was he who had asked for the meeting.

"Well," Alex said finally, "I have to get back to class in a few minutes, so . . ." He seemed to be looking at everything in the room except Philip. "I wanted to tell you that I've been offered the chance to study guitar in Spain, and I've decided to go."

"How long will you be gone?" Philip knew the answer didn't really matter but felt he should say something.

"A year. Maybe more." Alex nervously knocked the salt and pepper shakers together.

"When do you leave?"

"In May, as soon as classes are over."

Although that was more than a month away, Philip knew he would not see Alex again. "So that's it, huh?"

"Yeah." He nodded, as if to himself.

"Good luck," Philip said, trying to keep his voice steady.

"Thanks." Alex waited a moment, then stood to leave. Philip grabbed his hand. Alex slowly sat back down. They held hands across the table for a long time.

"Take care of yourself, OK?" Philip heard the words coming out of his mouth, but it was as though they were being said by someone else.

"You too." Their hands parted.

Philip watched Alex walk out into the street and kept watching long after he had faded into the cement and asphalt and the bustling midday traffic.

Interlude

Janna followed the narrow main road that curved through the hilly neighborhood of Manayunk. The faint scent of lilac drifted through an open window of the car. Blooming cherry trees decorated the landscape with blocks of white, pink, and magenta, stiff like open parasols atop dark, elegant trunks. Formerly consisting of dilapidated pubs and empty storefronts, the neighborhood was now an unending series of galleries, chic shops, and innovative restaurants. On spring weekends like this one, it was wall-to-wall people.

Janna parked her car and entered the restaurant where, for the past few months, she had been chef. After being her own boss, it was difficult to work for someone else, but she had no choice. As she had feared, expanding her café into the adjacent space had been a mistake. The business ran at a substantial loss for almost two years before she filed for bankruptcy. She wasn't happy about doing it, but at least this way she wasn't in danger of losing her home.

Her personal life was in as much disarray as her career. Shortly after Philip and Alex left, she ended things with Winston. She had been clinging to him like a life preserver, a confirmation of her normalcy. Once the boys were gone, she no longer needed him. While she accepted the demise of her relationship with Winston as inevitable, Philip and Alex's breakup devastated her. She knew what had happened wasn't entirely her fault. Maybe it wasn't even mostly her fault. But it made no difference. She had helped destroy the one thing in her life she truly cared about.

Since that time, Janna had been involved with only two other people. One was a brief, casual affair with a neighboring shop owner. The other was a one-time experience with an attractive Israeli lesbian. Although not in any way unpleasant, the dynamic of being with another woman lacked the spark Janna felt with men, or at least some men. Janna was glad she had been candid with the woman about her uncertainty from the beginning, so there were no hard feelings. Still, when Janna saw her now, she felt embarrassed, not for their shared experience, but for being so sexually adrift at her age.

Janna entered the kitchen. Her sous chef, Cynthia, eyed her over a tray of chicken breasts and remarked, "Don't you want to put on some lipstick or something?"

"Good morning to you too, Cynthia."

"Your boyfriend's here." Janna furrowed her brow quizzically as she hung up her jacket. "Don't pretend you don't know who I'm talking about," Cynthia chided.

"The carpenter with the stutter?"

Cynthia glared at her reproachfully. "If you're going to be rude, at least keep your voice down. He's right over us."

"Sorry," Janna said. "I didn't mean it that way. He seems like a nice enough guy."

"Nice, cute, and he likes you. So why aren't you doing something about it? And don't tell me it's the stutter, because that's barely noticeable."

Janna considered the question, but only momentarily. "He's virtually a child."

"Looks like a grown man to me. If he's a few years younger than you, all the better." Cynthia smiled wickedly. "He'll have more stamina."

"I hardly need someone with stamina the way my sex drive is these days."

"Maybe he's the guy to change that."

Janna didn't respond but conceded the point by disappearing into the rest room to fix her face. She wondered if she had really gotten desperate enough to chase after a manual laborer. She thought of her mother's adage, "If it's honest work, that's all that matters." She certainly agreed in theory. Reality, though, could be another matter.

Back in the kitchen, Janna placed a pitcher of ice water and a few glasses on a tray. After passing a self-satisfied Cynthia, she headed up the stairs. Approaching the second floor, she heard a mingling of rowdy voices, but when she entered the room, the men fell silent. Janna felt awkward, as if she were interrupting something. Her "boyfriend," as Cynthia called him, walked over, took the tray from Janna, and placed it on a workbench. "Thanks," he said with a disarming smile. "That was real nice of you." The other two guys began snickering. "George, Tom," he directed without turning around, "go out to the truck and bring in the rest of the planks."

"Yes, master," they intoned glibly, then left.

Cynthia was right, Janna thought. He was cute. Physical labor had honed his body in a way that weight lifting could never match. He had a boy-next-door face, with dazzlingly white teeth and a small, sun-burnt nose. The haircut was atrocious, but that was easily remedied. Janna allowed her eyes to drift away from him to survey the room. "The place is really coming along. How much longer before we can reopen the floor?"

"Two or three weeks."

The slight stutter that crept into his response made Janna ashamed of her earlier insensitive remark. "I know we've spoken a few times, but I don't think I've introduced myself. I'm Janna."

"Marty."

Janna repressed a grimace at the sound of the name, which immediately brought forth an image of Ernest Borgnine as the sad-sack butcher in the movie *Marty*. Surely there was something else she could call him. "Is Marty short for Martin?" she asked hopefully.

"Yeah, but everybody calls me Marty."

It had been worth a try. "So, Marty, how long have you been in this line of work?"

"On and off since high school."

"Then I take it you're not in high school anymore," she remarked wryly.

He laughed. "No, I'm not in high school anymore." His voice became teasingly coy. "I'm twenty-six. Is that what you wanted to know?"

Janna smiled and lowered her eyes, feeling pleasantly exposed under his gaze. So he was six years younger. That shouldn't be a big deal. It certainly wouldn't be if their sexes were reversed. "I bet you're one of those guys who built giant Lego skyscrapers when you were a kid."

"Skyscrapers, bridges, stadiums, you name it. I wanted to be an architect."

"My sister's husband is an architect. He likes it."

"It wasn't for me. I dropped out after two years of college. Couldn't stand sitting behind a desk all day."

There was a noise behind them. George and Tom were making their way up the stairs, teetering under a heavy load of wood. "Excuse me." Marty dashed past her. He lifted a bundle from the top of the pile and carried it effortlessly up the stairs. Janna knew it was stupid to be impressed by a man's strength, but she was anyway. "Well, I'd better get back to watching these goofballs," Marty said apologetically as he leaned the planks against the wall. "Thanks again for the water."

"Anytime."

"When are you two hitting the sheets?" Cynthia asked when Janna returned downstairs.

Janna briskly tied an apron around her waist. "He's too good-looking for me. Too young and too good-looking."

"Girl, get yourself some confidence! You're an attractive woman." Cynthia scrutinized Janna's ensemble. "Of course, you might want to rethink these pajama outfits you're always wearing."

Janna had never gotten over her adolescent habit of hiding her figure, and after so many years of defending her clothes to her mother, she had no patience for this. "Maybe tomorrow I'll dress like a hooker."

"Don't be so dramatic. All I'm saying is let the boy see what you've got."

▲▲▲

Although Janna didn't change the way she dressed, she started to pay more attention to her appearance, even waking up early to set her hair in hot rollers. She and Marty chatted throughout the day when the kitchen was slow, exchanging information about their families and childhoods. Marty was originally from the area, but when he was eight, his parents split up, and he moved to Phoenix with his mom and brother. His stutter had been worse back then, and it was difficult for him to make friends. Fortunately, by the time he reached high school, his aptitude in sports gained him popularity, and his stuttering eased. Now it seemed to surface only when the conversation turned personal, giving him a vulnerable quality that Janna found very attractive, especially in a man as seemingly confident as Marty. Janna was beginning to wonder, though, if the attraction was mutual. After two weeks of delicate flirting, he had yet to ask her out. Tired of waiting, Janna decided to take the initiative.

"Marty, would you like to have dinner together sometime?" she asked one afternoon when they were alone.

"Sure."

Janna thought he would take over the lead in making plans, but when he said nothing further, she continued. "When would be good for you?"

"Anytime."

"Do you have a favorite place or type of food?"

"Anywhere you want to go is fine."

It was clear she was going to have to orchestrate the entire evening. "Tomorrow's my day off. I'll pick you up at six and we'll go to the waterfront. How does that sound?"

"Good."

Janna didn't know what to expect after that exchange. He seemed pleased that she had asked him to dinner. Yet she wondered why he was so passive when it came to making the arrangements, not to mention why he hadn't asked her out in the first place. She hoped he wasn't one of those who just wanted to be friends. With that in mind, as well as Cynthia's advice, Janna rummaged through her closet for something less concealing than her usual attire. She changed her outfit five times before settling on a short, sleeveless blue dress. Although it was relatively modest, she still had to fight the impulse to pull a cardigan over it.

Janna arrived at the address Marty had given her, a row house in the working-class neighborhood of Upper Darby, just outside of Philadelphia's city limits. "Hi," he said brightly when he appeared at the door. "You look really nice. I mean, you always look nice, but . . ." He took a breath to ease his stuttering. "Thanks for coming."

He was wearing a button-down shirt and khakis, which bore the marks of having been recently pressed, and not by a professional. The image of him struggling with an iron for her was so sweet. She felt the impulse to kiss him right there, on the tiny cement stoop, but resisted.

He invited her in. The house was a disaster. Half the ceiling in the living room had been torn down, there was plastic on the floor, cans of paint, trays, and brushes scattered about, and two window frames propped up against a wall.

"Sorry about the mess. I'm doing renovations for my landlady."

Janna walked into the kitchen. The cabinets were in the process of being refinished. Half were covered with decades of peeling paint. The other half had been stripped, stained, and varnished. "What a difference," Janna remarked, thinking how good her kitchen cabinets would look with this kind of face-lift. A modern butcher block sat in a corner, out of place in the otherwise old-fashioned kitchen. The top was inlaid with tiny blue and white tiles arranged in a geometric design. "This is gorgeous," Janna said, running her hand over the polished wood. "Did you make this?" He nodded. "Do you know how much you could sell something like this for? Forget about refinishing cabinets."

Marty shrugged. "I like refinishing cabinets."

Janna started to laugh.

"What's so funny?" He asked defensively.

"You're very . . ." She stopped a moment to think about it. "You're very refreshing."

He looked at her guardedly. "That's a good thing, right?"

"Yeah, that's a good thing."

She asked to use the bathroom, which was upstairs. She hadn't intended to snoop, but when she saw the door to his bedroom ajar, she couldn't help but slip in for a quick look. There was an unmade mattress on the floor, no box spring or frame. A couple of boxes served as his dresser. She glanced in a half-open closet. The absence of women's clothing ruled out a live-in girlfriend, as well as transvestism. No pictures of naked men on the wall—another good sign. She remembered the days when she would have welcomed such pictures. Time to live in the real world.

Returning to the living room, Janna checked out his state-of-the-art stereo system, which was surrounded by crates of CDs. "Quite a music collection." She perused the titles. None were familiar.

"You like alternative music?"

"Uh . . ." She didn't know how to fake this.

"What kind of music do you like?"

Could she tell him that last week she spent an hour wandering around a used-book store because they were playing Neil Young's *After the Gold Rush?* She had long forgotten this collection of sorrowful songs about knights and queens, dark horses, burning castles, and broken harbors. But with the first few notes, it all came rushing back, reopening the raw wound of adolescence. She couldn't imagine explaining this to Marty, who undoubtedly had never heard the twenty-year-old album. Nor could she tell him about the silly disco songs from college she had detested when released but now listened to because they reminded her of friends who were gone. She decided to keep it simple. "I mostly listen to classical music."

"Oh." He paused. "That's cool." He scratched nervously at his temple, as though afraid she might try to engage him in a discussion on the subject.

"But I'm open to anything." OK, that wasn't exactly true, but it could be. She eyed some plastic shelving that held the only books she saw in the house. There was no literature, only architectural textbooks, an auto repair guide, and a few issues of a popular sports publication, including the renowned swimsuit edition. She had always found the effect this magazine had on certain men endearing. After all, the corner newsstand carried far more explicit material. Yet here they were, like little boys, looking at pictures of pretty girls in bathing suits. That Marty was one of these men only increased the tender feelings she was developing for him.

She noticed a small art reproduction taped to the wall. "You like Vermeer?" she asked excitedly.

"Huh?"

"Girl with a Pearl Earring." She pointed to the picture.

"Oh." His winsome smile twitched. "It was here when I moved in. I liked it, so I left it."

An affinity for Vermeer showed potential. "You should visit the Frick in New York. They have some excellent Vermeers. The rest of the collection is outstanding as well." Janna stiffened at the sound of her voice, fearing it was too professorial. But Marty looked at her as if she were the epitome of sophistication. It made her feel good about herself, a rare experience these days.

As they left his home, Janna's gaze was drawn to a flowering patch of land across the street, snuggled between two brick buildings. "That's a strange place for a garden," she commented, as it was the only greenery visible among acres of row homes.

"It was an empty lot. Some neighbors got together and fixed it up."

"Can we take a look?"

They strolled through the small, wild garden, passing bushes of red azaleas, orange tulips with yellow stripes, huge pink peonies, white bishop's bells, and mauve delphiniums. There was the most varied assortment of irises Janna had ever seen, some with velvet textures, others with scalloped edges, in regal palettes of purple, gold, russet, and peach. Arched over a wooden bench was a small weeping cherry, so fragile it looked like it would be felled by the first strong wind. Pale lavender wisteria hung from the side of an adjoining building. Vines of miniature pink roses climbed another. Janna carefully took one of the tiny buds between her thumb and forefinger. The intensely sweet fragrance rushed to her head like a drug. She held the flower up to Marty, enjoying the contrast of the delicate petals against his masculine features. He closed his eyes and inhaled, a look of voluptuous pleasure crossing his face. When he opened his eyes, Janna's gaze caught his. He blushed like a modest boy caught skinny-dipping by a pretty neighbor.

They drove to a restaurant at Penn's Landing and ate dinner while watching the ships in the harbor. Janna ordered a bottle of wine but drank only one glass. Since the fiasco with Philip and Alex, she had made it a point to cut down on her alcohol consumption. She did too many stupid things when she was drunk, and she didn't want to do anything stupid tonight.

After dinner, they walked along the waterfront to the historic old city area. They stopped at a corner to listen to a salsa band, then strolled along the colonial streets, glancing into shop windows. It was a clear evening, but it had turned chilly. He offered her his jacket. As he helped her into it, she felt his hands, big and protective, through the stiff denim fabric. She pulled it tightly around herself, soaking up the lingering warmth of his body. Whenever Janna had pictured the perfect man, she imagined someone different from herself, but usually in some superficial, glamorous way. Marty, however, was truly different—genuine and completely free of pretension. Although she found these qualities attractive, and thought (at least theoretically) that she should strive toward them herself, she wondered if she were really prepared to be with a man with whom she had so little in common.

The streets were nearly empty. Not ready for the evening to end, she invited him up for coffee. She left him in the living room with some Chopin nocturnes while busying herself in the kitchen. When she returned, he was sitting on the couch, looking as anxious as a fifth grader waiting to be called into the principal's office. She sat next to him, setting the coffee service on the table. Neither one of them touched it. If ever there was a time for him to make a move, this was it. Yet he simply sat there. She decided to take the plunge. "Marty, are you involved with another woman?" She was about to add "or man" but thought better of it.

"Oh, no."

"Are you attracted to me?"

"Of course," he said emphatically.

That was a nice touch. "Do you mind that I'm older?"

His stutter, which had almost disappeared in the last few hours, returned full force. "No, I like that." The tension in the room soared, crackling between them like static electricity. Janna's gaze fell to a dark freckle nestled in the soft curve of his lower lip. It looked like it had been tattooed there, just below the skin. All evening she had wanted to touch it. Now she did, with the tip of her finger. Then she leaned forward and kissed him. He responded, but not in the way she expected. He kissed back, and ardently, but did not put his arms around her. Instead, he closed his eyes and relaxed into the couch, as if waiting for her to continue. She did, and within minutes he was flat on his back and she was crouched over him. She didn't know how they ended up in that position, but they both seemed to gravitate toward it naturally.

She sat with one knee on each side of his leg, feeling nearly naked in her thin dress. She slipped her fingers between the buttons of his shirt, feeling bits of skin, then popped them open to run her hand across his chest. For one moment, infinitesimally brief, she felt like a man. Or rather, what she imagined a man would feel like in her place. Before she could fully grasp the sensation, it was gone, leaving her with a weird, wide-awake feeling. She watched him, his eyes still closed. His arousal was evident. It wasn't just that he had an erection. His heartbeat was racing, and his whole body seemed to pulsate. Yet he was utterly still, as if his arousal had immobilized him. She knew he was waiting for her to make the next move. Although excited by his expectation, she forced herself to stop. If they went any further they would end up in bed, and she didn't want to do that, not on the first date, not with a guy she liked this much.

"Marty?" He opened his eyes, looking up at her with startling boldness. "It's getting late, and I have to be at work early tomorrow." It was the truth, but it felt false. "Do you mind if we call it a night?"

"No," he said with a heavy stutter. He didn't try to convince her to let him stay, as other men would have. She liked that. But she sensed something was wrong. He was averting his face as he buttoned his shirt. Perhaps he thought she was rejecting him for his passivity, as undoubtedly other women had.

"When can I see you again?" she asked, hoping to make her intentions clear.

He turned to her, astonished. "You want to see me again?"

"Very much." She touched his face and could not resist another kiss. Unable to stop, she finally said, "Let's go upstairs."

Once in bed, they fell back into the position they had been in on the couch, with her on top. Undressing him slowly, she delighted in the sight and feel of each newly exposed part of his body. When he was naked, she looked at him spread out and felt something ignite inside her. Shucking off her clothes, she straddled his waist, just teasingly out of reach of his penis, which she was pleased to see was not oversized. She liked the way he responded to her caresses, murmuring as she stroked his chest, nibbled his nipples, and licked the sensitive skin at the edge of his armpits. His hands remained on her back, as if unsure whether they had permission to venture elsewhere. Having such a big guy at her mercy was so exhilarating. It was like what she had felt with Philip and Alex, only better, since now she was a participant instead of a spectator.

She scooted a few inches down, rubbing herself leisurely against him, flooding the pleasure center of her brain. Lowering her head, she nuzzled, then sucked his neck. He gave a muffled moan that became more audible as she increased the pressure, until she was sure he'd be black-and-blue the next morning. Lifting her head, she found an expression on his face she had seen only once before, on Philip as he was about to be penetrated by Alex. Only this time the expression of ecstatic submission was for her. At that moment, she felt a convergence of every incomprehensible erotic feeling she had ever had, from her lifelong fascination with gay men, to the impossible desire she'd had for Alex that day at the beach. It all seemed to make sense now, although not in any way she could explain. Placing her lips over his open mouth, she felt his breath mix with hers. Then she reached for a condom, rolled it onto him, and eased herself down after it. He was quiet but kept his eyes on hers until the moment he came. The force almost knocked her off.

"Are you OK?"

"Yes, yes," she said as he drew her to his side and they relaxed against each other. After intercourse she always had the feeling of something being over, but it was another one of mother nature's tricks. He had felt good inside her, and they were a nice fit, but she needed more. She stepped into the bathroom to clean up and pee. He'd better not fall asleep while I'm in here, she thought. Returning, she found him sitting up, with the sheet demurely pulled over him. In the dim light, he could have been Philip. He and Alex had been the last men in this bed, and the image of them still burned in her memory.

Marty snuggled against her like an orphaned pup, his head on her slim shoulder. "Janna, I want to . . ." He stopped and started again. "I'll do anything you want, but you have to put me there." Janna was not sure if he had said put or push, but it hardly mattered. Then, as though pleading with a benevolent queen, he added, "P-p-please." Janna found herself incredibly aroused. What intrigued her the most was the muscular, self-assured quality of his submissiveness. It didn't seem in the least an outgrowth of inexperience or timidity. Equally captivating was this sudden, exaggerated shyness—whether intended for his own erotic pleasure or hers, Janna did not know.

What a peculiar boy, Janna thought, as she placed her hand on the top of his head, stroked his hair, then pushed him firmly down to her breasts. Although his body language continued to be sweetly bashful, his mouth was not. The sensuous brush of his lips and tongue, mixed with the rough graze of his stubble, made her feel like every nerve in her body was standing on end. When the pleasure became too intense, she pushed him down farther. She could sense how excited he was. His tongue was teasingly soft on the outside of her body, surprisingly hard when he pressed it inside. He went back and forth like that, inside and out, until she was gripping great fistfuls of sheet in her hands. Then she felt the ridge of his teeth against her opening and his tongue flickering above. She cried out as a giant wave of pleasure hit her, followed by smaller ones, until every last pulse of feeling had been wrung from her. Exhausted, she released the grip of her thighs.

"That was wonderful," he said, embracing her hips. He lay across her abdomen for a moment, then sat up suddenly. "I almost forgot." He reached over the side of the bed, rummaged in his pants pocket, and pulled out one of the tiny roses from his neighborhood garden. Although crushed and wilted, it still had a muted scent.

"How sweet." She held the flower to his nose, hoping to see that look again on his face. It was there, but it paled against the more intense expressions she had seen in the last hour. Cuddling against him, she was surprised and flattered to find him erect again. After waiting for the sensitivity in her pelvis to subside, she pushed him playfully on his back and reached for another condom.

"Janna, we don't have to."

"I know. I want to. Don't you?" This was not entirely true, but she didn't mind and felt he deserved it.

"Yes, but—"

She leaned over, pressing her finger to his lips. "Then be a good boy and stop talking."

The Calm After

Philip released the thumbtack from the corkboard in his kitchen, allowing the ticket to drop into his hand. When he had seen the notice of Alex's performance, he knew right away he would attend, although he pretended to consider it for a few days. He tossed the ticket onto the coffee table, next to the photo album that contained the few pictures he had of Alex. Although Alex usually mugged for the camera, there was one shot Janna had taken that was really nice. Alex was leaning against Philip and had this huge, vibrant smile. Philip looked at the picture for a long time, then turned to an old box of cards, letters, and other souvenirs from their relationship. He picked up a snow globe Alex had given him one Christmas and shook it, watching the white flakes swirl around the tiny town. He ran his hand along an expensive scarf, paisley silk on one side, wool on the other, which Alex had given him for his twenty-first birthday. Philip had never worn it for fear of losing it. He recalled the pleasure of opening the slim box, of Alex placing the scarf around his neck and kissing him. How strange that out of the thousands of kisses they must have exchanged, Philip remembered that one so vividly. He opened a purple plastic Easter egg, pushing aside bits of artificial grass to pull out a scrap of sheet music on which Alex had written "I love you." Philip smoothed the torn edges of the paper, then carefully tucked it back in the egg.

~~~

It was 1997, seven years since he had last seen Alex. Following their breakup, Philip finished college, then moved to Princeton, where he took a job with a satellite design firm. Then he met Kurt. Philip was initially attracted to him because he was so different from Alex, both in looks and personality. Blond, muscular, and easygoing, Kurt shared a number of Philip's interests, such as running and racquetball, and they got along well. After they had been dating a few months, Philip invited his sister Jeannette to come to Princeton to meet him.

"What did you think?" he asked as they walked to her car.

"He's fine."

"Just fine?"

"What do you want me to say? He's not Alex." She slipped into the front seat of her car. "When is Alex getting back from Spain, anyway?"

"He's already back."

"You've seen him?" she asked excitedly.

"No. I've heard, from friends."

"Well?"

"Well what? Am I supposed to drop everything and go chasing after him? What makes you think he even wants me to?" He stopped her before she had the chance to respond. "You know what? It doesn't matter. I've moved on with my life. I'm with Kurt now, and I'm going to try to make that work."

"Do whatever you want," she said irritably, slamming the car door shut, "but don't expect me to come all the way out here again for some gym bunny."

He did try to make things work with Kurt, but as time passed it became clear they were better suited as friends than lovers. Sexually they were a bad match, with everything a compromise, and neither of them getting what they wanted enough of the time. Something was missing emotionally as well. At first it was a relief not to experience the intensity of feeling he had with Alex. But after six months Philip began seeing other men. He told himself it was not cheating because they weren't committed, but he was not being up-front with Kurt, and that felt wrong. When he came clean, Kurt admitted that he, too, had been seeing other guys, although he was evasive about whether it had been recently or throughout their relationship. There seemed no point in continuing, and they separated amicably.

After Kurt, Philip hooked up with a series of lanky, boyish guys who bore a general resemblance to Alex. Although he hated to admit it, this was now his "type." Each of these short-lived relationships, if they could be called that, ended when Philip or his boyfriend of the moment found someone who was more tantalizing simply by virtue of being new. Philip's emotional life fell into a holding pattern, and he began to wonder if he would ever have another long-term relationship. Then he met Drew. Five years Philip's senior, Drew had sandy blond hair and a fabulous smile. They were a good match all around, and for the first time since Alex, Philip felt he was falling in love. After six months, Philip found a job in Philadelphia and moved into Drew's apartment. The only point of contention was Drew's career. A senior litigation associate with a large Center City law firm, Drew worked unceasingly. On weekday evenings he frequently didn't get in until after Philip was asleep. Weekends weren't much better. The only time that was sacrosanct was Friday, their designated "date" night. It simply wasn't enough. Philip hated seeing Drew come home exhausted, and he didn't want to add to his stress by making additional demands on his time, but he felt increasingly ignored and unappreciated.

Making a conscious decision to act responsibly, Philip suggested counseling. Drew agreed but had to cancel so often because of his job that it made little impact. A further strain was added when, during an argument, Philip accidentally called Drew by Alex's name. There was dead silence, then, "Who's Alex?"

"What?"

"You called me Alex."

"I did?" Philip shook his head. "I'm sorry. He was my first boyfriend." Although this wasn't actually true, it was how he always thought of Alex.

"Why have you never mentioned him?" Drew asked suspiciously.

"It never came up."

"Where is he now?"

"Damnit, Drew, I don't know. I haven't seen him in years. He has nothing to do with what's going on between us."

"Maybe not. But when we're discussing our relationship, I'd appreciate it if you'd remember which boyfriend you're talking to."

Things went downhill from there. After two years together, they parted. Philip regretted how things turned out but felt this time he had done everything he could.

A year had passed since then, and Philip had met no one he was interested in. He had continued counseling on his own, hoping to understand some things about his behavior that had troubled him, chiefly why he had sabotaged his relationship with Alex. The mess with Janna, a bad idea all around, was supposed to be solely for her, but Philip found he got something out of it too. Not that having her there improved sex. If anything, it inhibited them. But although he hated to admit it, his vanity was flattered by the idea that someone wanted to watch them make love. Philip never would have allowed another man to watch. He was way too jealous for that. A woman seemed nonthreatening, and less sexual, perhaps because female sexuality was such a mystery to him. Kissing Janna was sheer stupidity. He chalked it up to things you do when you're young and drunk, but he knew that did not excuse it. The irony was, he and Alex would have gotten over the kiss, eventually. It was Philip's explosion into violence they couldn't overcome. It had taken him years to admit responsibility for what had happened. He hoped that by doing so, and by learning better ways to deal with his anger, he would avoid making the same mistake with other men. But that was minor consolation.

᭝᭝᭝

Philip waited until the lights went down before entering the auditorium, to avoid the chance of Alex seeing him from the wings. A third of the theatre was empty, which was dispiriting given the small size of the room. When Alex stepped onto the stage, though, the enthusiasm of the audience's applause made up for its limited number. Alex smiled and bowed gracefully. He was remarkably unchanged. Philip almost wished it were otherwise. It would have made it easier.

The evening consisted entirely of guitar pieces written by Alex. Some had an exuberant flamenco beat. Others were languid and introspective, leaving Philip with a vague sense of longing for something he could not quite define. That longing was supplanted by quiet exultation during the last piece, a brief but sublime work aptly titled "Halcyon Days." The crowd was silent for a moment after the final chord, then erupted into applause.

As the audience dispersed, Philip slipped into the men's room. He fiddled with his hair in front of the mirror, trying to cover the beginnings of a receding hairline. Figuring one handicap was enough, he slipped off his glasses. After looking around the blurry men's room, he returned the frames to his face. He straightened his turtleneck, buttoned his suit jacket, then unbuttoned it again. Suddenly he felt foolish. He didn't even know if Alex would see him. Exiting, he searched for the backstage corridor. He walked toward a man standing alone near a lit doorway. As he got closer, he recognized Alex's father. "Mr. Everett," he said, extending his hand. "How are you?"

Alex's father tentatively shook the outstretched hand. Then, a flash of recognition crossing his face, he clasped Philip to his chest and patted him on the back. "Helen," he called to a woman facing away from them in the doorway, "look who's here." Alex's mother turned, revealing a face that had aged greatly since Philip had last seen her. She pressed his hands in hers. "How wonderful to see you, dear. Does Alex know you're here?"

"Not yet."

At that moment Alex stuck his head out of the room. "Mom, do you know if . . ." His eyes widened. "Phil?"

"Hi," Philip said lamely. They were about ten feet apart. Neither of them moved to close the distance. "I saw the notice about the performance in the paper. Hope it was OK for me to stop by."

"Sure." Philip thought he detected a note of hesitation but wasn't certain. "A few friends are here if you'd like to come in." Upon entering Alex's tiny dressing room, Philip's throat constricted. Two young women were speaking to an attractive older man who Philip immediately assumed was Alex's lover. But Alex introduced him as a former teacher, and the man's stiff manner and quick exit assured Philip there was nothing more between them. The women left, and they were alone. Alex leaned against the counter that jutted out from a mirrored wall, diminishing the effect of his superior height. They locked eyes, and Philip gazed into the pure, perfect blue of Giotto's scenes from the life of Christ.

"How are you?" Philip asked nervously.

"Good, good." Alex nodded. "And you?"

"Good."

"That's good." Alex crossed his arms over his chest. "This really is a surprise."

Philip fumbled for something to say. "I recognized some of the pieces tonight from the CD you released last year."

"So you're one of the five people who bought it."

"Yeah." He smiled self-consciously. "Your work is always so amazing. I never know what to say."

"Philip, why are you here?" Alex asked gently.

Philip looked around the room, as if the answer lay in one of its dusty corners. "I don't know," he confessed. "I guess I was hoping we could go for a cup of coffee or something." When Alex didn't respond, he realized this whole thing had been a mistake.

He was about to turn away when he heard, "Give me a minute to get out of my tux."

Philip was startled by Alex's appearance when he emerged from the room. He had automatically expected to see him in his old uniform of jeans, T-shirt, and sneakers. Instead, Alex was dressed like an adult, in loose wool trousers, a finely knit sweater, and real shoes. Although a minor thing, it was a telling sign of how much time had passed.

On their way out, they stopped to say good-bye to Alex's parents, who had been waiting down the hall. Alex handed them his garment bag and guitar case. "I'm going out with Phil for a while." These simple words struck a deep chord in Philip.

"Have a good time," Alex's mother said.

Alex's father shook Philip's hand. "It's good to see you, son. Don't be a stranger."

Outside, Philip asked, "Don't be a stranger? Do your parents remember who I am?"

"Times change," Alex said thoughtfully. "Even parents grow up."

Philip suggested a cozy restaurant where they could talk, but Alex had another place in mind. Following Alex's directions, Philip drove to a loud, bustling diner in South Philly. It had the appearance of one of those retro diners, but it was the real thing, there since the 1950s. They slid into a booth and perused the menu.

"So, how long are you in town?" Philip glanced at Alex's impressive legs, which spilled into the aisle from beneath the table.

"Indefinitely."

This was far better than Philip had expected. "Where're you living?"

"I've been staying with my parents since I moved back from New York. But it's been a few weeks now. I need to start looking for an apartment."

"You were living in New York? Last I heard it was Madrid." That was a lie, but Philip didn't want to admit how long he had known Alex was back in the country.

Alex gave him a puzzled look. "I was only in Madrid for two years. Then I came back to Philly to finish my degree. I thought you knew that. In fact, I kind of expected to hear from you then."

"I didn't know you wanted to hear from me."

Alex shrugged. "I guess I could have called you too."

An aging, beehived waitress took their orders. Once she left, Philip asked, "So, what brings you back home?"

"There are too many distractions in New York. I can't get serious about my work if I'm partying every night. Things have already gotten back on track. I'm working on an opera about Garcia Lorca, mixing in scenes from his play *Bodas de sangre*—Blood Wedding. The play is about impossible love, and Lorca was gay, so there are wonderful parallels." Alex's voice grew animated. "At the end, after Lorca is shot by the fascists, there'll be a fantasy sequence, restaging the flight scene from the play, only this time the lovers will be two men, and they'll escape instead of die. Sort of a metaphor for the survival of Lorca's work after his murder."

"Sounds interesting."

Alex continued at rapid speed. "This is only the beginning. I have so many ideas. I've been taking it too easy, doing these little guitar études."

"But they were superb," Philip protested.

Alex waved his hand dismissively. "I can write those in my sleep. I need something challenging. I was disciplined in Spain, but I've gotten lazy."

"What was it like living there?"

"A lot of work, but an amazing experience. I studied with some of the greatest guitarists in the world. Then I come back here, and the guitar is treated like a novelty instrument."

"How about a career as a violinist? It's a popular instrument, and you play remarkably."

"Now you sound like my father," Alex said peevishly as the waitress set down their food. "I'm not interested in being a concert artist. The competition is brutal and would leave me no time to compose. Anyway, I don't want to waste my life in hotel rooms and airports. I do have to find a way to make a living, though. The commissions aren't exactly pouring in. You wouldn't believe the stuff I did in New York. I played at weddings and society parties where old, drunk guys hit on me. I gave violin lessons to six- and seven-year-olds, whose nannies would dutifully report the mothers' belief that their little Johnny or Jane was the next Jascha Heifetz. You haven't lived until you've heard that name pronounced with a Jamaican accent. When things got really bad I even waited tables. Unbelievable."

Alex was in his own world, speaking at Philip rather than to him. But then he leaned toward Philip and said, "Sorry for blathering on like this. So much has happened in the past—how many years has it been, anyway?"

"Seven," Philip answered without hesitation. He had already done the math and wasn't going to pretend he hadn't.

"That long?" Alex gazed off into the distance. Philip couldn't read the expression on his face. "So, what have you been doing all this time?"

"Nothing too exciting. Got my degree. Got a job in Princeton. My company was purchased by another company and I was unemployed for a few months. Then I found a job in Valley Forge and moved back here."

"What do you do?"

"I design thermal systems for satellites."

"I have no idea what that means, but it sounds impressive. Do you like it?"

"It's OK. I have to be in the office by the crack of dawn. I travel to places nobody wants to go. My boss is a dimwit. The usual stuff." He paused. "I've thought about starting my own consulting business. I could set my own hours and probably make more money. But I don't know if I'm ready for that yet."

"You will be, eventually."

Philip watched Alex's lips close around a straw. They were the color of faded roses and could still make him hard from across the table.

"How's the family?" Alex asked.

"Everyone's great. Jeannette's a pharmacist, and she's engaged to a terrific guy. Simone's in law school and François is a freshman in college."

"You're kidding! Last I remember, François was a little kid."

"Believe me, he still is."

"How's your mom?"

"Good. She got remarried recently. I threw a tantrum until Jeannette clued me in on what a jerk I was being. I wish they hadn't sold the house, though."

"That's too bad," Alex said with a hint of wistfulness. "We had some good times there."

"Yeah, we did." It seemed as good a time as any to broach the subject Philip had wanted to raise all evening. "Seeing anyone these days?" Alex shook his head. "Well," Philip continued, awkwardly attempting a joking tone, "I'm sure you've left a trail of brokenhearted lovers across the globe."

"A few ersatz boyfriends, maybe, who probably haven't noticed I'm gone. I'm not really the type to have lovers." He took a sip of coffee. "You were the exception." When he lowered his cup he stared into it for a long time. "You know, Philip, maybe it's a mistake to have a relationship like ours when you're so young. Everything after that . . . well, you just expect too much."

Philip drove Alex to his parents' home. They walked in the cool night air toward the front door, stopping as if by habit just outside the reach of the porch light. This was where they used to say their good-byes, kissing until the hour became ridiculous, or a noise in the house threatened the appearance of a parent. It was reassuring to Philip that, after so many years, this shadowy spot still retained its magical quality. "This was nice," Philip said. "Can we do it again?"

"I don't think that's a good idea."

Philip was jarred out of his nostalgic fog. "Are . . . are you saying you don't want to see me again?"

"Things have changed. I've changed."

"I know."

"No, you don't. You really don't."

Philip took a step toward him. Alex backed away into the porch light.

It was late when Philip got back to his apartment, but he was too wired to go to sleep. He puttered around, feeding the cat and picking out his clothes for the next day. It was only when he sat in his too-bright kitchen, sorting through the mail, that he felt the true weight of his loneliness.

A week later, to Philip's surprise, Alex invited him to a basketball game. Although it was hardly the most intimate of settings, Philip accepted, glad for the chance to see him again. At first, they were having a good time. The game was engaging, and in the slower moments they amused themselves by picking out the worst-dressed members of the audience. During the third-quarter break, Alex left, ostensibly to get a soda. By the time he returned, sodaless and without an explanation for his lengthy absence, the game was over. The ride back home was nearly silent. Philip rolled down the windows to let in the cool night air and tuned in a jazz station. As they neared Center City, he asked, "You want to go for a drink or something?"

"No thanks."

Philip resigned himself to the fact that this was going nowhere. Alex picked up one of the CDs lying on Philip's dashboard, a Chet Baker album. "Can I?" he asked. Philip nodded, remembering how they had discovered Baker together, ten years ago, in a small arts cinema. Prior to the feature was a black-and-white short. An aging wreck of a man sat alone in an empty studio and sang, a cappella and painfully slowly, a plaintive plea to his lover to take him back. The broken, anguished voice had mesmerized them both. Later, they stopped by the jazz section of a record store and picked up a few of his albums. Again and again they listened to the timeless tales of love and loss, waltzing clumsily to the songs, laughing as they tripped over each other's feet.

Alex flipped the disk into the deck and played with the buttons. He selected an early recording in which Baker, his voice then young and fluid, fondly recalled the great love of his life: "I remember you, you're the one who made my dreams come true." Philip stiffened in his seat, wondering if Alex were trying to tell him something, or if he had randomly selected the song. They pulled into the driveway as the song reached its conclusion. "When my life is through, and the angels ask me to recall the thrill of them all, I'll tell them I remember you." Philip put the car in park. "Nice choice."

Alex exited the car without responding. Philip shook his head in confusion. Leaning into the window, Alex said, "Sorry about tonight. Let's do something later this week, OK?" Driving home, Philip tried to make sense of the evening. Giving up, he pushed the CD back into the player and keyed up "I'm a Fool to Love You."

Philip waited a few days and then called. "I thought, well, if you're free Saturday, maybe you'd like to come over for dinner."

"You know what I'd like to do instead? Go to the Barnes museum."

Philip was silent for a moment. "OK." First a crowded, noisy, ultra-straight diner in South Philly, then a crowded, noisy, ultra-straight basketball game, now an art museum on a Saturday afternoon. What next, the Flower Show on Mother's Day?

Once they reached the museum, Philip's assessment changed. It had been years since he had been to the mansion on Philadelphia's exclusive Main Line. The museum was neither crowded nor noisy, due to its stringent restrictions on the number of daily visitors. They walked peacefully through the small, intimate rooms, discussing the magnificent canvases that packed each wall, or simply stood before them, awestruck. The shock of the new never left these masterpieces, and Philip delighted in seeing them as if for the first time.

Exiting down the marble steps into the suburban afternoon, he felt a unique closeness with Alex from having shared such immense beauty. It was still early, so Philip suggested that they pick up a couple of sandwiches and go to Kelly Drive. As they walked through the park that bordered the Schuylkill River, Alex gathered brightly colored leaves that had fallen from the autumn trees and twisted their stems together. "What are you doing?" Philip asked.

"I was trying to make you a whimsical crown, but I never was very good at arts and crafts. Here." Alex dropped a handful of leaves on Philip's head. "Kind of the same effect, don't you think?" he asked blithely.

Philip brushed the leaves off his head and tucked a few in his breast pocket. When they had first met, he had spent many lunch periods with Alex sitting among the fall leaves in the school graveyard. He vividly recalled how he ached to touch Alex then but was afraid to, things being so uncertain between them. Here he was, more than ten years later, reliving those same emotions. As Alex walked ahead, Philip let his eyes linger on the back of his body, the side he often faced when they made love. It was hard for Philip to look at him now without seeing Alex naked under him, without remembering the creaminess of the skin on his ass, the insane excitement of Alex parting his cheeks, the ecstasy of entering him. He was overwhelmed by the desire to be inside him now, not to fuck him, just to be there, to be home again.

They sat on the grass, side by side. Alex opened his sandwich and, after taking a bite, picked out something with a green border. "What do you think this is?" He showed it to Philip. "An apple?"

Philip bit off a piece and grimaced. "No. Jicama. Maybe."

Alex threw it to the ducks. "That's what I get for ordering a 'gourmet' sandwich." They watched rival crew teams race on the river as they finished their lunch. "It's nice being in a park without having to fight for a place to sit. I missed that in New York. I missed the seasons too. Last year I visited my parents in May just to see the dogwoods in bloom."

Philip unbuttoned the flannel shirt he was wearing as a jacket and tied it around his waist. Out of the corner of his eye he caught Alex glancing at his T-shirted chest. When their eyes met, Alex abruptly looked away. Damn, thought Philip, he's going to make me pay for that. He wondered why Alex was intent on hiding his attraction when Philip had made his abundantly clear. He was the one who had searched out Alex, and his intentions must have been so obvious that Alex had yet to ask whether he was involved with anyone. Despite this, Philip could feel Alex bracing for an offensive assault. It came with even greater force than he expected.

"New York still has Philly beat in a lot of ways, though," Alex said glibly. "Sex, for example. So many men. I thought I'd never be able to get through them all."

"So that was your goal, to 'get through' every man in the city?"

Alex chewed on a blade of grass. "Not *every* man. Not the ones I found unattractive. But that didn't narrow the field much, especially when you're in a club so dark you could be having sex with your father and not know it."

"Charming." Philip knew he had no right to be upset, but he was.

"At least anonymous sex is honest. Nobody promises to call you the next day when they know perfectly well they won't."

"It's not the anonymity I have a problem with," Philip said, although that was hardly true. "It's the excess."

"Well, excuse me for enjoying my sex life." Alex's voice clouded with anger. "Did you think I had been celibate since we broke up?"

"Of course not."

"Or maybe you thought that upon your return I would confess how empty my life's been without you, and that I can't have relationships because I think about you all the time. And wait, this is a good one." He raised his hand to punctuate the statement. "When I have sex with other men I pretend they're you. Is that what you wanted to hear?"

Although stung by the vehemence of Alex's sarcasm, Philip knew there must be some truth in what he said, or else he wouldn't have been so vicious. "I know I shouldn't be judgmental. I really want to understand."

"What's there to understand? I enjoy meaningless sex, and I try to enjoy it as much as possible. That hardly sets me apart from the majority of other men on the planet."

"But if that's your preference, why were you with me so long?"

Alex poked the ground with a twig. "I didn't say it was my preference."

They sat in silence a moment.

"Did you do it when you were with me?" Philip asked.

"What?"

"Were you with other guys?"

Alex groaned. "Is that what this is about? No, Philip, I was not. How could I be? You were up my ass practically twenty-four hours a day. There was hardly time for anyone else to be there."

Philip decided not to press the issue, especially given his own undisclosed infidelity at the end. It would be the height of irony if Alex, who claimed not to care about sexual fidelity, had remained faithful, while he, an advocate of monogamy, had not. Yet Alex was not completely free of hypocrisy either. He had been jealous at times, accusing Philip of flirting with other guys, not to mention flying off the handle when Philip kissed Janna. Perhaps everyone needed the comfort of their personal myths, Philip thought, whether they fully believed in them or not. His was one of monogamy, Alex's of sexual freedom. But the fact was that as men they were predisposed to desire sex with more than one partner, and as humans they were predisposed to jealousy if their mates acted on the same impulse. The trick was finding the balance between the two, or perhaps accepting that there was none.

"Alex, I need to say something to you. I've never forgiven myself for what I did . . ." he began, and then forced himself to say, ". . . for hitting you."

Alex crushed a brittle leaf in his hand. "You weren't the first. You weren't the last."

Philip let the pain of this truth sink in. "I know I can never make it up to you. But I hope one day, if I try real hard, maybe you'll be able to trust me again."

They sat hugging their knees, watching the river reflect a riot of color from the setting sun. The cooling air was filled with the soft snap of acorns hitting the ground. The park was nearly empty. The crew teams rowed leisurely back to their boathouses, now outlined with strings of white lights against the approaching night.

Alex stood up. "Your offer for dinner still good?"

Philip had imagined that the first moment they were alone in his apartment, they would be all over each other, but it didn't happen that way. By the time Philip wrested his temperamental key from the front door, Alex was halfway across the apartment, examining the sterile furnishings of the living room. He walked to the picture window. "Nice view."

After Alex had stood staring out of the window for some time, Philip said, "Guess I'll start dinner."

"Why is this so hard?" Alex asked abruptly.

He considered the question. "Maybe we're both scared."

"What are you scared of, Philip?"

"That it won't be like the way it was."

"Yeah. That must be it." Alex nodded thoughtfully. "Let's not put too much pressure on ourselves, OK?" Alex's glance fell to his calf, where Philip's black and white tabby was butting her head. "Is this Mioche?" he asked with happy surprise, picking her up. "I can't believe she's still alive."

"She's an old lady, but she's hanging on."

"It's nice to see something familiar." He petted her contemplatively. Philip walked over, took Mioche from him, and set her down. He placed a hand on Alex's shoulder and let it fall down his arm. They embraced, and the impact of Alex's chest against his stung with loss and remembrance. A moment later they were kissing wildly, their hands rushing to shatter the years of their separation. Philip guided them into the bedroom and onto the bed, without once separating his mouth from Alex's. He began undressing Alex as rapidly as possible. "Wait," Alex said. "We need to talk first."

"About what?" Philip murmured, not slowing his pace.

"Safe sex."

"I'm always safe. You know that."

Alex stopped him. "You need to hear me on this. There were things we did before that I don't do anymore."

Philip sat up on the bed in silent resignation. "Sorry. I'm listening."

"No oral sex without a condom, which I think makes it pointless, but if you want to do it that way, I will."

Philip gave a small sigh. "I can live without it. I can live without almost anything, as long as you don't tell me I can't fuck you."

"Well, actually . . ." Philip's breathing stopped. Alex grinned. "You should see the look on your face." After a brief silence, they both cracked up laughing. Philip was thinking how good it was to hear Alex's laugh again when it ended abruptly. Sensing something was wrong, he stroked the side of Alex's face. "Is there something else?"

Alex was silent for a long moment. Then he cleared his throat. "You'll use a condom during sex, right?"

"Of course."

Pause. "And no rimming."

"How about if I just put my tongue—"

"No."

"But—"

"No."

"OK," Philip conceded.

"And, I hate to say this, but we need to cool down the kissing before one of us splits a lip."

"All right. Is that it?"

"Yeah. I guess so." They resumed kissing, a little more calmly, finished undressing, and got into bed. Lying side by side, they reacquainted themselves with each other. Alex leisurely stroked Philip's thigh. "I can't believe how good you look. You still have the best body of any guy I've been with, and believe me, that's saying a lot." Philip looked slightly wounded. "Hey, that was a compliment."

"I know. I just don't like to be compared with other men. It makes me feel, I don't know, like they're in bed with us."

"There's only one person who's ever been in bed with us, and it wasn't a man."

Touché, thought Philip. "I'm really sorry about that."

"It was my fault too. I should have been clearer about what I wanted. Let's not talk about that. The only thing I'm interested in is us, here and now."

"Sounds good to me." Philip rolled Alex on his back and examined his body in an almost clinical manner. It was the same and yet different from what he had remembered. Although still slender, it had lost its teenage gawkiness and gained a bit more muscle, which Philip found pleasing. He traced a finger along the thin line of hair that ran from Alex's belly button to his sternum. "This is new," he purred, pulling playfully at the sparser hairs coiled around Alex's nipples.

"Good or bad?"

"Everything is good. Better than good." Philip lowered his body onto Alex's. This simple act was the most pleasurable moment in sex for him, short of orgasm. Perhaps it was because they touched so fully in that position, even more so than during intercourse. Whatever the reason, the feeling had lost none of its intensity in the years they had been apart. Alex slipped his legs out from under Philip and wrapped them around him. Philip thought of how close he had come to never again experiencing this moment, to never again seeing Alex as he was now, stretched out under him, extravagantly relaxed in his arousal, eyes unflinchingly focused on Philip, waiting for him to break the barrier of flesh between them. Philip rolled away to get a condom from the nightstand. As he rooted around in the drawer, he felt Alex's hand on his arm. It was not a caress; it was a signal to stop. "Phil?" Alex said in a shaky voice. Philip turned to him apprehensively, trying to ignore the fear that had been building in him. "What's the matter?" he replied, his mouth so dry he could barely speak.

"There's something I have to tell you."

Philip froze. No, he thought, please no.

"I should have told you before, I was trying to tell you before, but . . ." Alex said nothing more. Philip pulled him close, and with Alex's face wet on his shoulder, managed to string together a few stock phrases of comfort. "Don't worry. Everything will be OK.

I'm here." In the hour that followed, silent but for Alex's intermittent, soft crying, Philip thought about what this meant, for the both of them. He had read about men who spent years of their lives taking care of dying lovers. But they were heroes, and he did not feel like a hero. He looked down at the head on his chest that rose and fell with each breath he took. He knew he loved Alex and wanted to do all he could to keep him as healthy as possible for as long as possible. This he would do whether they were lovers or friends. What he didn't know was how he would get out from under the curtain of grief that surely would fall once Alex was gone.

The traffic noises had quieted down to an occasional whoosh of a lone car. It was raining. Alex stirred, lifting himself from Philip's chest. "Do you have a tissue?"

"Sure, baby." Philip handed him the box.

"No one's called me that in a long time." He blew his nose. "Actually, no one's ever called me that but you." Philip felt a twinge of guilt. "Baby" was his standard endearment in bed. Like everything else, though, it felt different with Alex. "Listen. My doctor's pretty sure I was infected recently because my T cell count is so high, but he thought you should get tested anyway, to be on the safe side. It's up to you, of course."

"I've been tested a few times. So far, I'm negative." Philip felt almost ashamed saying this, like it was a boast, but Alex, clearly relieved, simply said, "Thank God."

"You talked to your doctor about me?"

"Of course. You were the first person I thought of."

"Really?"

"Even if we weren't in contact, I never stopped caring about you. You were the best friend I ever had. You were the best anything I ever had."

Philip thought about how different things could have been. A tear slid down the side of his face. "I know it was my fault we broke up—"

"Please, Philip. This doesn't help."

"But if we hadn't broken up—"

"Stop it!"

Philip did as Alex asked but silently blamed himself. He found it more comforting than facing the fact that there was no one to blame. "At least your T-cell count is high."

"It'll buy some time."

"That's important. They're coming up with new treatments left and right." A thought flitted in Philip's head, one he was too frightened to verbalize. Maybe there would be a cure in time. Maybe things would be all right.

"They've got me on some stomach-turning stuff now. I spent the first few weeks on the toilet. It's better now, but I still have reactions sometimes. Like that night we went to the basketball game."

"Oh."

"Yeah. That's what that was about. Anyway, I'm not sure I should continue taking it. I'm sicker with it than without it."

"Don't do anything without talking to your doctor. Maybe get a second opinion." He stopped. "I'm sorry. I don't mean to be telling you what to do."

"I'll take all the help I can get. You should see my mom. She's an expert on all the new treatments. She actually interviewed doctors for me."

"It's good that she's there for you."

Alex was silent a moment. "Better late than never."

Philip stroked his back. "It's getting late and we haven't had dinner. Why don't I throw something together?"

"Thanks. I don't have much of an appetite, but I'm not supposed to skip meals these days."

Later they sat surrounded by dirty dishes at the kitchen table. "That was fun, like an indoor picnic," Alex said.

"I would have warmed it up if you'd given me the chance."

"Guess I was hungrier than I thought."

"I'd offer you more chicken, but it looks like someone else has her sights on the leftovers." Mioche sat upright on one of the kitchen chairs, greedily eyeing the carcass. "I'd better go feed this animal."

When five minutes had passed and Philip had not emerged from the kitchen, Alex stuck his head in. Philip was babbling in French to Mioche while dumping some kind of powder into a food processor. "I thought feeding a cat was opening a can and putting it on a plate. What are you doing?"

"Mioche is on a special diet for her kidneys. It's a little more work, but she's like a kitten again." Philip placed her bowl on the ground. Mioche dived in.

"You're a good mother," Alex said, smiling. "I never would have believed it."

"Close your eyes."

"Why?"

"If I tell you, it's no fun." Alex lowered his eyelids. Philip pressed his lips firmly against one and then the other.

"I had forgotten how good that feels," Alex murmured. "Do it again." Philip did.

"I'd still like to make love, if you want to," Philip said when Alex opened his eyes.

"Are you sure?"

"Yes."

"But I'm afraid, well, you know what I'm afraid of."

"We'll be very careful."

"There's still a risk. You know that."

Philip nodded, but deep down he was scared. He knew he took a chance every time he had sex with someone. It was different, though, when you knew your partner was infected. Once he was about to go home with a man he met in a bar but backed off when the guy disclosed his HIV status. Philip felt bad about punishing the guy for his honesty, but he was not willing to take that kind of a risk with a stranger. Alex wasn't a stranger, though. He was the man Philip had once hoped to spend the rest of his life with, and now he would have to be satisfied with whatever was left.

Back in bed, Philip held Alex's head tight as their bodies moved together, communicating in their ancient, familiar language. A longing grew in him, reaching far beyond the physical into a place frightening and glorious. Tears threatened to well up again. Perhaps it would have been better, he thought, if Alex had waited until afterward to tell him. He would have liked to have made love to him at least once without this crushing heaviness in his heart.

If he was going to start crying again, he didn't want Alex to see it. Philip pulled himself up into a sitting position and guided Alex into his lap. Wrapping his arms around Alex from behind, Philip whispered, "You still like it when I hold you like this?"

Alex smiled. "Yeah. Makes me feel real close to you."

"And me to you."

Philip pressed his fingertips against the sides of Alex's torso, steadying him as he rocked in Philip's lap. His fragile joy was shadowed by a heavy sadness. His thoughts drifted to all the things he would never experience with Alex again. How he would never again fill his mouth with him, feeling him alive at the back of his throat. How he would never again be penetrated by Alex. Although it was not something they had done often, he would miss that part of Alex, and of himself. He would also have to abandon the fantasy of one day being able to make love to Alex without a condom. It was especially maddening to think they could have done it before, when apparently both of them were negative but were too frightened to take the test. Back then Alex had asked Philip repeatedly to put it in "just for a minute" without a condom. Philip gave in a few times, but his paranoia was so great he remained inside only long enough to realize the pleasure he was missing. He had hoped that one day they would be able to commit to each other completely, test negative, and engage in all forms of sexual activity without barriers or fear. But that was not to be.

Philip rested his chin on the back of Alex's shoulder. In the past he would have gently chewed on it, but now he satisfied himself by running his lips over the fine muscles there and blowing hot breath in Alex's ear. "Are you cold?" Philip asked, as they were completely uncovered.

"What? No," came Alex's raspy reply. After that the room was silent except for their breathing and the sound of rain spilling out of a drainpipe. Philip's hand moved to caress the hard center of Alex's chest. He reached to Alex's small, taut nipples, stroking them until Alex moaned softly, leaned his head back, and pressed himself further down onto Philip. Philip's fingers wandered to Alex's outstretched throat, then to his mouth, tracing his full lower lip and slipping in to touch his teeth. Alex opened his mouth, drew in two of Philip's fingers, and sucked hard. Philip was flooded with the sensation of being completely inside Alex. At the same time, he felt Alex inside him, in a wholly different but no less significant way.

As they sped toward the end, Philip tugged his fingers out of Alex's mouth and wrapped them, slick with saliva, around Alex's cock. At least, he thought, I can still have him here, hot in my hand. He anticipated the small happy murmur Alex used to make when he came. Instead, Alex emitted a guttural moan that tore Philip out of his momentary bliss and plunged him back into sorrow. A cold terror formed at the base of Philip's spine, threatening the loss of his erection. Not able to bear the thought of such an insurmountable precedent, he finished quickly, shocked, when it came, at the sweet punch of pleasure so at odds with his emotions.

The next morning Philip felt confident enough to face Alex when they made love. This time the sadness, although still present, remained at the corners of his consciousness, and he was able to enjoy himself a little more freely. Afterward, he prepared breakfast trays of waffles and fruit, and bowls of scalding, milky coffee topped with brioche crumbs, a favorite of Alex's from the past. Philip was pleased to see him eat so heartily. Although he adored Alex's lean frame, he wanted to get some weight on it, insurance for the future. Once the trays were cleared, Alex snuggled down in bed. "You'd better watch out. I could get used to this."

"I wish you would."

Alex looked at him, suddenly wary. "Let's not rush into anything, OK?"

"I don't want to rush you. I'm just hoping for another chance."

Alex rubbed his eyebrow. "You know, Phil, I only found out
about this thing a few months ago. I'm still learning to deal with it.
Are you sure you can?"

"I wish you didn't have it. I can't lie about that. But it doesn't
change the way I feel about you. That's never changed. And I don't
want to delay things between us anymore."

"You mean now that there's not much time left?"

"No," Philip said quietly. "That's not what I meant."

Alex pulled his knees up to his chest and nestled his chin against
them. "Let's just see how things go."

As they lay in bed that afternoon, talking, joking, and fooling
around, Philip finally felt at peace. Please, he thought, a prayer directed to a god he was not sure existed, I'm willing to do anything.
Please don't let this end.

Coda

Janna leaned into the backseat to make sure Alex was strapped in comfortably. "Wooby," Alex demanded indignantly.

"Where's her wooby?"

"In the trunk. S-sorry." Marty got out of the car, handed the toddler her stuffed rabbit, and kissed her tiny silken head.

Janna looked at the clock on the dashboard. "Just once I'd like to be on time for church."

Marty flipped the ignition. "I'm sure your parents saved us seats."

Janna had never thought she'd willingly set foot in church again, having had her fill as a child. But it was important to her that Alexandra be exposed to Ukrainian culture, and the church was their strongest institution. She especially wanted Alex to learn the language, which she associated with the love and comfort of her grandparents. So she took a brush-up course to improve her pronunciation and asked her parents to speak Ukrainian around the baby as much as possible. She felt bad, though, that Alex would soon be speaking a language her own father didn't understand. Janna supposed this was one of the reasons her parents had been insistent she marry a Ukrainian. Fortunately, by the time Janna announced her engagement, her parents were so thrilled she was marrying anybody that they didn't utter a word of protest. As it turned out, they seemed to genuinely like Marty. Her father even approved of his being her junior, saying young men make more babies. So far he had made only one, but she was perfect.

Marty's proposal, though long in coming, was wonderfully spontaneous. They had stopped by an ice-cream shack on their way to a weekend at the beach. Sitting on a rusted bench, sharing a vanilla cone with crunchies, Marty sprang the question, and without a hint of a stutter. She was so surprised that her fingers lost their grip on the cone, which landed wet in her lap as she accepted. They had been involved for three years, living together for two. It had reached the point where she was considering proposing herself. She had been the instigator in every other aspect of their relationship. Janna's gut told her, though, that she'd have to leave this step to him. A man has to know he's ready to get married, and that only happens when he hears the words coming out of his mouth. But it was a very long wait. It wasn't that Marty was afraid of commitment. He had been the first to confess his love, within the early weeks of their relationship, and was elated when Janna asked him to move in. The problem was his passivity, which, though delightful in the bedroom, could be annoying outside it. He had no problem being assertive at work, or with his buddies, but when it came to the two of them, she was the decision maker. In general, she was happy with the arrangement. There was no issue about where they were going to live, what school Alexandra would attend, or how they would invest their money. Whatever Janna decided was what they did. There were times, though, when she wanted his assistance. Then his pat answer of "whatever you want is fine" was irritating. In the balance, though, it was a windfall to have such an easygoing husband.

Before she met Marty, Janna had always feared that too much satisfaction would bore her. When she thought about that now, it made her laugh. Her life wasn't perfect, no one's was. But when she looked at Marty and Alexandra she felt a happiness in the center of herself that made everything else seem unimportant. Of course it was different from single life, which was full of the excitement of endless possibilities. But when you win the marathon, you're relieved it's over, even though you might fondly recall some of the highlights of the race.

They had driven only a few blocks when, glancing out the window, Janna saw two men walking down the street. As they came closer, she squinted, unable to believe her eyes. "Stop the car," she ordered.

"What's the matter?"

"Nothing. Just stop." She opened the door before the car came to a complete halt. "Wait," she called, walking briskly after the two men. They turned. "Tell me I'm not dreaming." She flung herself into Alex's and Philip's arms. Stepping back, she held their hands and marveled at how mature they looked. "When did this happen? How did this happen?"

They both started talking at once, then Philip deferred to Alex. "I moved back to Philly about a year ago, and this one, a glutton for punishment, tracked me down."

"So you're friends again?" Janna asked tentatively.

"More than that." Philip lifted Alex's left hand with his to display their matching bands. The burden that had weighed on Janna for so long was lifted and replaced with a bright joy.

"In fact," Alex said, "we just returned from the South of France, where we were honeymooning." He turned to Philip. "Ooh, I like how that sounded."

Philip looped his arm around Alex's waist. *"Nous sommes dans le ravissement."*

Alex eyed Philip suspiciously. "Did you just say you were going to ravish me?"

"I think he said you're in a state of rapture." Janna pulled the translation from her high-school French.

"Very good," Philip said, "although Alex's interpretation has its appeal."

It was touching to see how frisky they remained with each other after all this time. And there was something new, a mellowness and sense of security. "Married," Janna declared. "I can't believe it. I would have loved to have been at the ceremony."

"It was private," Philip responded carefully.

"I understand, family and close friends." Janna was disappointed, but then, she hadn't invited them to her wedding.

"No, the two of us kind of private."

"Oh." Janna felt her face flush as she tried to reign in her imagination.

"It looks like you haven't done so bad yourself," Alex commented, looking toward her car. "That is, if the hunk and the adorable baby are yours."

Janna smiled proudly. "Can't believe I did it, huh?"

"What I can't believe is that you found a straight man you could stand," Philip teased. "He is straight, isn't he?"

"No, he's a bisexual hermaphrodite. Come on and let me introduce you. Then we need to run. We're late for church."

"Late for what?" Alex choked back a guffaw.

"They let you in a church?" Philip exclaimed with mock horror. *"Quel scandale!"*

"It's been how many years, and within five minutes you're tag teaming me," Janna grumbled. She walked toward the car with the two of them following behind. Marty stood on the pavement, leaning into the open car, playing with the baby.

"Cute ass," Alex whispered.

Janna was going to reprimand him, but instead she said, "Yeah, and he's all mine, so hands off." Marty straightened up as they approached. "I'm sorry I ran off like that, honey. These are two very dear friends I haven't seen in . . ." she began and then looked at them ". . . well, too long." Strange how she still considered them friends. They had been in her life only a short period of time, and years ago. Yet she continued to feel a strong connection with them. The men shook hands and exchanged greetings as she made introductions. She pulled out her ruddy-cheeked, golden-haired tot from the car, smoothing a few pieces of hair out of her face. "And this little angel is Alex, short for Alexandra."

"That's a funny coincidence," Marty said, casually gesturing toward Alex. "You and the baby have the same name."

Janna could feel Alex's eyes on her. She held out the baby to him. He took Alexandra into his arms and swung her around airplane style until the bright peal of her laughter filled the street. As he passed the child back to Janna, he smiled, and she felt another burden lifted. They said their good-byes, exchanging hugs and handshakes, phone numbers, and promises to keep in touch. Yet even as she slipped out of their embrace, Janna knew, with a mixture of sorrow and relief, that if she saw them again, it would be like this, an accident. Janna wondered how long it would be this time—five years, ten, twenty?

As Marty strapped the baby into the car seat, Janna watched the two of them walk into the distance, hand in hand. In the middle of the block they stopped to exchange a kiss. Of all things, it reminded her of the first time she saw them kissing, in her dream. She still found it beautiful, and it made her feel good and calm and excited all at once. And maybe a little nostalgic. What was thankfully missing was the painful longing she used to feel. She longed for nothing now.

ABOUT THE AUTHOR

Juliet Sarkessian is a Philadelphia-based writer and lawyer. She lives in domestic bliss with her partner of sixteen years and their twenty-year-old cat. *Trio Sonata* is her first novel.